"Everything is g...
Gabe moved to ...
against him.

His arms felt so good ...
"You can't be sure of that. We still haven't found the killer."

"I'm sure as anyone can be of anything."

"Why?"

"Because I believe in you." He drew back enough that he could see into her eyes. "I believe in us. Together, we'll find proof—"

"You believe in us?" she echoed, her heart thumping against her ribs.

"We make an unstoppable investigative team."

"Oh." She thought Gabe was getting to something more intimate. It certainly felt as if it should be, her being in his arms with his body pressed against her, hips to hips, breasts to chest.

"I thought maybe you meant something more personal," she said, unable to stop herself.

Gabe's low, sexy voice vibrated through her when he asked, "Do you want it to be more personal?"

Available in June 2005 from Silhouette Intrigue

Undercover Encounter
by Rebecca York
(New Orleans Confidential)

On the List
by Patricia Rosemoor

Sheikh Surrender
by Jacqueline Diamond

A Dangerous Inheritance
by Leona Karr
(Eclipse)

On the List
PATRICIA ROSEMOOR

SILHOUETTE®
INTRIGUE™

First published in Great Britain 2005
Silhouette Books, Eton House, 18-24 Paradise Road,
Richmond, Surrey TW9 1SR

© Patricia Pinianski 2004

ISBN 0 373 22791 4

46-0605

Printed and bound in Spain
by Litografia Rosés S.A., Barcelona

PATRICIA ROSEMOOR

To research her novels, Patricia Rosemoor is willing to swim with dolphins, round up mustangs or howl with wolves—"whatever it takes to write a credible tale." She's the author of contemporary, historical and paranormal romances, but her first love has always been romantic suspense. She won both a *Romantic Times* Career Achievement Award in Series Romantic Suspense and a Reviewer's Choice Award for one of her more than thirty Intrigue novels. She's now writing erotic thrillers for Mills & Boon Blaze.

She would love to know what you think of this story. Write to Patricia Rosemoor at PO Box 578297, Chicago, IL 60657-8297, USA or via e-mail at Patricia@PatriciaRosemoor.com, and visit her website at www.PatriciaRosemoor.com.

CAST OF CHARACTERS

Renata Fox—The bright, young Safenet agent thinks her agency got the wrong man accused of being the Chicago Sniper. Now someone wants *her* dead, and only a mysterious stranger can help her.

Gabriel Connor—The elusive Team Undercover operative has his own secret reasons for wanting to protect Renata and prove her sniper theory is correct.

Muti Hawass—He's been identified as the Chicago Sniper, then shot dead. But is he the real killer or another innocent victim?

Tag Garvey—A sharpshooter with Safenet, why is he suddenly harassing Renata?

Frank Broden—The Safenet agent supports Renata, but is that just a cover to get close to her and end her quest for justice for good?

Elliott Mulvihill—The director of Safenet has ordered Renata to cease her inquiry or she could lose her job.

Thanks again to Sergeant David Case for giving me some insight on police procedures and relationships between local police and federal agencies.

Prologue

Who would be the next victim?

For nearly a week now, Chicago residents had been keeping to themselves, venturing out of their homes only to go to work or to perform some necessary task. Even then, they'd looked over their shoulders, wondering who the City Sniper would stake out next. Some believed the shooter was a psychotic with a god complex, but the majority believed he was a terrorist, drawing attention and manpower to the shootings while more widespread plans were afoot.

Good.

Standing back from the apartment window so he wouldn't be seen, he laughed to himself. Below, the head of S.A.F.E., which stood for Security Agency Fighting Extremism—a Homeland Security operation—signaled the uniformed men to scramble into position. He spotted two sharpshooters taking position on the roof opposite and knew there would be more men overhead that he couldn't see. They were there because the authorities had pinned the identity of the sniper who killed citizens seemingly at random.

Seemingly being the operative word.

Believing they had the killer in their grasp, they thought they were going to take him down. *Fools!* A well-placed phone call had set up the bogus confrontation exactly as he'd hoped.

The men below scurried around like ants, so cocksure of themselves. Oh, they would get their supposed sniper—a known suspect already under government surveillance. They would even find their proof.

But they wouldn't find *him*.

The shootings would stop, though, and the authorities would pat each other on the back, certain they'd gotten their man.

The area below was still.

No movement...no sound...as if the city were holding its collective breath.

And then he heard the door below opening.

He steeled himself to stay where he was, away from the window, so he wouldn't draw attention to himself. He wanted the focus to remain right where he'd centered it.

Then he saw him. Muti Hawass scurried along the courtyard sidewalk, a long package in his hand. One long enough to hold a weapon.

He raised his own and watched the man through his scope.

"Stay where you are, Hawass!" came a shout from streetside.

Hawass froze, then pulled a handgun and blasted away as he tried to make a run for it.

He smiled. The patsy had played right into his hands.

Several cracks from various points reverberated through the courtyard and Hawass stumbled, the package dropping from his hand. Then the man dropped, too, face down in the courtyard, brains and blood splattering the sidewalk around him.

Dead...no doubt there.

Exactly as planned.

Chapter One

"'Elliott Mulvihill, director of S.A.F.E., the newest arm of Homeland Security, denies allegations that Muti Hawass wasn't the City Sniper,'" Gabriel Connor read. He snapped the morning newspaper open and went on.

"'The proof is in the aftermath,' Mulvihill said. 'The sniper took five lives, a new victim every other day for nearly two weeks. And a week has gone by since he was unfortunately killed, and there hasn't been another incident.'

"'The denial comes in response to a report filed by Agent Renata Fox. When questioned by a WBNX reporter, Fox told all. She found information in the histories of the victims that indicated the shootings were *not* random, after all.'

"'And if something so important about an investigation is off, then it's time to look at all the facts again,' Fox maintains."

Having relayed the story in a nutshell, Gabe lowered the newspaper to look at his boss. They were in

Gideon's Club Undercover office—all black and chrome furniture and deep blue walls. Gideon himself reclined with his feet up on his desk, looking more relaxed than he had since Gabe had first met him several years before when they'd both needed new identities.

"So what do you think?" Gabe asked.

"That Agent Fox's theory has at least enough merit to question the case."

"That's what I thought."

Gabe knew that Fox had followed her gut and had taken another look at the case files after Hawass was killed. She'd noticed that each of those victims had something off in their histories. Not one average, law-abiding John Q. Citizen among them. So she'd questioned whether there might be a criminal connection that took the shootings out of the terrorist arena and therefore out of Muti Hawass's hands.

Meaning, the sniper was still out there...

"Mulvihill had a lot of nerve stopping her report from going further," Gabe said, his voice bitter. "I don't blame Fox for blowing the whistle on him." She'd been the darling of the media—and no doubt the pariah of S.A.F.E.—for the last twenty-four hours, Gabe thought.

Gideon pinned Gabe with his intense blue gaze. "It's not the shooter who interests you."

"Nope."

"And it's not that you feel sorry for Fox, either."

"You're on a roll."

"It's Mulvihill."

Gabe nodded. Gideon knew his background. Not many did. Not many men Gabe could trust with it. Like souls, they'd bonded the first time they'd been thrown together, and the rest was history.

Maybe that's why, when he'd been at loose ends and wanting a friendly face six months before, he'd looked up Gideon here at Club Undercover. Now Gabe was settled in as Club Undercover's security chief. And on the side, he'd helped Gideon and his team with a couple of covert operations, as well.

Club Undercover…when the desperate have nowhere else to turn…

"So what do you have in mind?" Gideon asked.

"I'm going after Mulvihill, of course. I'm going to find out whether or not the director of S.A.F.E. pushed the task force in the wrong direction as Agent Fox indicated. And if he did, I'm going to make sure he gets nailed."

At least for his latest crime.

"And your plan is…?"

"Use the woman to get to him."

FEELING LIKE the wind had been knocked out of her sails in the past twenty-four hours, Renata Fox stared out of the S.A.F.E. office window and wondered if she'd made the biggest mistake of her life by blowing the whistle on the agency. More specifically, on Elliott Mulvihill.

"He says my judgment is impaired," she told Agent Paul Broden, one of the few employees who seemed willing to speak to her today.

Broden was a little under six feet tall, with a body that appeared more agile than pumped. His thinning blond hair and three-piece suit added to his quiet command. They were in his cubicle—hers didn't have a window. Being one of S.A.F.E.'s top agents, he got sunlight and a view of other Chicago Loop office buildings and pedestrians scurrying along the streets below. Too bad his legendary dedication to the job had lost him his family. His wife had blamed their teenage son's problem with drugs on an absent father and had divorced Broden shortly after Renata had joined the agency.

"You *are* new at this," he reminded her.

"I was hired for my skills," she said, meeting his steady gray gaze that held just a touch of pity.

She'd only joined this S.A.F.E. office that summer after training in Virginia. And before that, she'd been a corporate mediator with an advanced degree in psychology. This was her first job in law enforcement, and if she'd ever wanted to be part of the good-old-boy network, she'd just put herself squarely out of the running.

"But the task force didn't need a negotiator in this case."

"But they needed a good psychologist. That's why Mulvihill gave me open access to the files. He should have given me those files sooner than he did. It all happened too fast. And Muti Hawass wasn't the sniper," she added for good measure.

"I know you believe that." Broden drummed his long fingers on the desk. "No one's been shot since he was put down."

"Put down?" she echoed, taken aback by the phrasing.

"Like a rabid animal. Hawass was no innocent. He was already on the watch list. Even if he's not the sniper, that doesn't mean he's never killed anyone."

Renata gaped at him. "That's cold, Broden."

"That's realistic. Consider the background we have on Hawass. Consorting with known terrorists, being picked up several times for suspected terrorist activities. We just never could get the goods on him."

Renata knew other law enforcement people had the same attitude—letting an offender who got off on one crime pay for another seemed to be okay with them.

"What about justice?" Renata asked.

"Keep in mind Hawass was no innocent and you'll feel better."

But no, she really wouldn't, Renata thought, which probably made her as naive as she was green.

"I know what it's like to make a mistake and hold unpopular opinions," Broden stated. "But the agency hasn't recovered after the Embry Lake fiasco, and here we are with another potential problem."

Months before she'd been hired, the Embry Lake standoff in Michigan had echoed the FBI's Ruby Ridge incident. Nine civilians had been killed, starting with militia leader Joshua Hague.

"This is no Embry Lake," she insisted.

"You're right. And people here will come around. You need to hang in there until things die down. In the meantime, drop this whistle-blower thing, Renata, for the sake of your career. Your first big assignment and you've made a powerful enemy."

Renata sighed. Director Elliott Mulvihill had looked right through her that morning. "I appreciate your not turning your back on me, Broden."

"Hey, everyone makes a mistake. I'm just giving you a pass on this one."

But she hadn't made a mistake, Renata thought, as she traded Broden's cubicle for her own.

She would bet her career on it.

She *had* bet her career on it.

Though she couldn't be fired for going over the director's head and speaking out, there were other ways to punish her, to make her quit. But she wasn't going to quit. She couldn't let her family be mired in humiliation and disgrace again. She'd heard the anxiety in her mom's voice when she'd called that morning. Renata had assured her mom that she would be all right. That her career would survive.

But would it?

That remained the uppermost worry on her mind as she checked her messages—another from her mom, the rest from reporters who were hoping to make a name on her back. Not that she was going to cooperate. The only call she intended to return was her mother's.

Tapping into her speed dial, Renata took a few deep breaths and pasted a familiar smile on her face, hoping it reached her voice.

"Hey, Mom, what's up?"

"Renata, honey, reporters have been calling here all morning. And I think one is outside waiting for me to leave the house. What do I tell them?"

"Don't talk to any reporters, Mom. You don't have to. Maybe you should go visit Aunt Lainie until this passes over."

Her mom wasn't strong like she was, Renata knew. The publicity and the effect on her family was the only thing she regretted about going public with that report. It brought up terrible memories for them all, but worst for her mom. Linda Fox had never gotten over what had happened to her beloved husband—she'd had a breakdown over his death. But her dad had instilled such strong ethics in Renata. She'd had to do what her conscience directed.

Voice trembling, her mom said, "My home is here."

"Okay, then stay here. Don't let them chase you away. Maybe you could just stay inside for a few days."

Renata spent a few minutes engaging her mom in a non-work-related subject until she was sure the older woman was more at ease. Then she signed off and got to work. Not wanting to run into any more reporters herself, she waited until after-hours that night to leave the office, when only a skeleton crew was left to watch her progress out of the cubicled area to the front door.

Not one of them said so much as a word to her.

She was waiting for the elevator when Director Mulvihill came out of his office. Surprised that he was here so late, Renata was doubly surprised when

Congressman Carl Cooper walked out behind him. Cooper was head of the government committee that had given S.A.F.E. its charter, and he was also under indictment for misuse of government funds. The two men conferred for a moment. Then Cooper looked up and spotted her. She'd never met the man, and he didn't look friendly now.

Flushing, Renata realized Cooper knew who she was. She was glad when the elevator doors opened and she could escape his glare.

More down than she'd felt in years, Renata left the building with a cold feeling in her chest and an ache in the pit of her stomach.

So when she hit the street—this part of the Loop being near deserted right after rush hour—she was trying to decide what she could do to make herself feel better. Dinner and a movie?

More like takeout and a rental.

"Agent Fox," came a smooth voice from directly behind her, "can I buy you a drink?"

Starting, she whipped around to face a dark-haired man who topped her by half a foot and had leather-encased shoulders broad enough to make her wary. Though she tried to mask the frisson of unease that rippled through her, she stepped back and put extra distance between them.

"I don't drink with men I don't know. And how do you know who I am?"

Ignoring the question, he smoothly said, "The name's Gabriel Connor. Gabe. I thought we could talk about the City Sniper over a drink."

"A reporter?" She shook her head. "Sorry, I'm talked out on the subject."

But when she started to turn away, he grasped her arm. He didn't hurt her, but he held her in a way that it would take some effort to free herself.

"I'm not a reporter."

"Let go of me," she said, turning her voice steely. "And don't touch me again without my permission."

He grinned then, which softened his expression, and let go. Lights from the building revealed smile crinkles around long-lashed green eyes. His other features, topping a dark green cable-knit sweater and tan leather jacket, were more rugged; his square chin beard-stubbled. He was very attractive.

"So what would it take to get that permission?" he asked softly.

Was he really flirting with her? Ignoring the little flutter in her stomach, Renata shook her head and turned her back on him to go.

As she started to walk away, however, he said, "I want you to know I believe you…"

She slowed her step.

"…and I want to help you prove Hawass wasn't the shooter."

AGENT RENATA FOX turned to face him, her expression a mask of incredulity.

Gabe stared, fascinated by her exotic beauty. Thick dark hair and high cheekbones indicative of a Native American ancestor warred with eyes that glowed like sapphires. Her nose was a narrow straight slash, but her full lips were curved, though she wasn't actually smiling. She was wearing a blue wool suit—not a pants suit, but one with a skirt that showed long, shapely legs—and shoes with high heels and sling backs that were just to the left of sensible.

"I don't get it," she said, her voice low and smooth like honey. "Why would a stranger want to help me? What's in it for you?"

"Does something have to be?"

"I would say…yes."

"Why?"

"Because people don't offer to do things for other people out of the goodness of their hearts."

"I'm not people," Gabe insisted. "Why don't we talk about it over a drink."

He thought she was going to say no, but then her suspicious expression lightened just a hair and he figured something changed her mind.

"A drink wouldn't hurt anything." she said. "Actually, I could use one after the day I've had."

Gabe let her take the lead and for a moment enjoyed the view from behind.

She chose a bar on the first floor of a nearby hotel. The place was classy and dark. They slid into one of the booths near the window and gave the waitress their orders—a shiraz for her, a beer for him.

She waited until the waitress was out of earshot before asking, "So who are you really, Gabe Connor?"

If he told her the truth, that would be the end of the conversation. So he told her the part of the truth that he could share.

"I run security for a club in the Wicker Park/Bucktown area."

"A security guard."

"No, the one who hires them. Maybe you've heard of it—Club Undercover."

Renata shrugged. "Sorry. I don't do clubs."

In an effort to get her relaxed, Gabe told her a little about the club and how it combined dancing with performance art. All the while he wondered what Renata would think if he told her about his involvement with Team Undercover, as they jokingly called themselves. Under Gideon's direction, he and the others helped out people in dangerous circumstances, when they had no one else to help them.

The waitress returned with their drinks and Gabe told her to run a tab.

"To the truth," he said, lifting his beer. "And by the way, in addition to running security for the club, I'm also a patriotic American."

"Then you should be pleased with Muti Hawass's death."

Gabe went still. "I would never wish death on someone who didn't deserve it, who was simply in the wrong place at the wrong time."

She blinked and something registered in her dark eyes. Then she shuttered any expression, asking, "How do you know he didn't deserve to be shot?"

"If you were comfortable with that, you wouldn't

have looked for another answer. An unpopular answer at that."

"Popularity contests never impressed me. And so far, neither have you."

She was impressing the hell out of him, though, Gabe thought. "You don't believe I want to help you."

"I believe you have a reason for *wanting* to help me," she said, pulling out her cell phone and playing with the keypad. "I just haven't figured out why."

"Well, believe this. I'm good at getting information from all kinds of sources."

Though she didn't look up from her cell phone, she lifted one delicate eyebrow. "So you're a private investigator, as well?"

"I'm a lot of things...or have been." Suddenly annoyed that she was only giving him half her attention, he asked, "Do you need to do that right now?"

"Check my messages? Yes."

Watching her long, slender fingers work the pad of the cell phone, Gabe wondered if she was going to make her calls right then and there. Why not? She'd already interrupted their conversation.

But it seemed that she hadn't lost a beat when she looked up and said, "You almost intrigue me."

A real multi-tasker...

"Almost?" he repeated.

"It comes down to this, Mr. Connor—"

"Gabe," he cut in to remind her.

"Gabe, then. You're a civilian." She slid the cell back into the safety of her shoulder bag. "The City Sniper is government business."

"Justice is every American's business."

"I'm glad you feel that way."

"The problem is I don't believe in justice."

"You don't believe in justice or just the system?"

"The concept sounds good, and sometimes the system works. But too often it doesn't and criminals are never made to pay. So make a believer of me," he challenged her.

"I'm sorry," she said, reaching into her pocket and producing a twenty-dollar bill. "I don't see that you have anything to offer me." She stood. "And even if you did, you would complicate things further. My life is too complicated as it is." She slipped the money between their glasses. "Drink's on me."

"I'm sorry you feel that way," Gabe said, not about to give up so easily. He slid his card toward her. "In case you change your mind." He thought she might not bite, so he turned on the charm, giving her his best smile. "I'm available to take care of all your needs."

Seemingly unable to help herself, she allowed her features to relax in a smile that lit her from the inside out. Gabe stared, entranced.

"All right," Renata said, taking the card and slipping it into her purse. "I'll keep it in case I have any needs that must be met."

"Good. I'll be waiting for your call."

So HE'D BE WAITING for her call, would he?

Not knowing why she'd even picked up Gabe Connor's card, Renata smiled wryly as she set off into the dark for home.

Home was a Wabash Avenue building with shops on the first floor. The upper floors, formerly offices, had been converted to studio and one-bedroom apartments. The building catered mostly to students attending the half dozen colleges with downtown campuses. Though not exactly glamorous, her apartment was an affordable five-minute walk from work.

As she crossed the street, Renata thought about the card burning a hole in the shoulder bag pressed between her arm and her side. Not to mention the intriguing man who had challenged her to take it.

She couldn't involve Gabe in S.A.F.E. business—she could only imagine what she'd pull down on her own head if she was so incautious. Mulvihill would probably find a way to use any variation from standard procedure against her, and she didn't need any more ill will from his direction.

As to her other, more personal needs...well, they could wait. Yes, she found Gabe Connor good-looking, but no, she didn't need a distraction at this point in time.

Turning onto Wabash, she closed her ears against the screech of metal on metal—wheels on tracks—as a train braked overhead.

The one drawback to her living situation, probably the rationale for the rent being so reasonable, was the location of the El—the elevated rapid transit system that circled Chicago's business district and gave the Loop its name. The century-old steel-and-wood structure ran overhead, straight down her street. Even inside her apartment, she could hear the constant clacking of running trains and the screech of brakes, no matter what the hour.

Away from State Street and the theater district, her area was nearly deserted at night except for a handful of people coming and going from the nearby station. And so, as always an alert city girl, she kept watch on her surroundings.

She didn't miss a thing.

Not the car inching along, its driver obviously hoping for a parking space to magically appear.

Not the well-dressed woman who hung out on the corner, nervously glancing up the street, apparently waiting for a ride.

Not the laughing trio of teenagers who swept down the opposite side of the street to disappear around the corner.

With her doorway just ahead, she let down her guard long enough to imagine what it might be like to laugh with Gabe Connor like that.

Just long enough to have someone come out of nowhere and dart at her from behind.

Chapter Two

Adrenaline surged through Renata, and the sound of her blood rushing through her ears muffled the slap-slap of feet against the cement sidewalk behind her. Before she could turn to face the person, cruel hands dug into her shoulders and shoved her into the closest recessed entrance to a shop.

Gasping, she forced herself around and caught a flash of a knife.

She reacted instantly, stomping her heel on the man's foot hard enough to put it through flesh and possibly bone. Heavy leather stopped her from eliciting more than a surprised grunt from her attacker, but she followed up with an equally forceful hand, her shoe smacking into the face encased in a dark hoodie. No damage there, either, since he turned his head with the strike.

Still, he spat, "Die, bitch!" in a dark, low voice, and she knew she had to get out of this *and now* to survive.

If she didn't throw up first...

Somehow, she anticipated his knife and placed her

shoulder bag between it and her body. The sharp weapon cut through the leather like butter, but the metal inside stopped the blade from slicing her open. Before he could recoup, she elbowed him hard, shoved her shoulder into his chest and freed herself from the doorway.

Moving faster than she knew she could, Renata unzipped the side of her shoulder bag and withdrew her weapon.

She could hardly breathe but she yelled, "Bullets trump blades!" and aimed the Glock at him. "Drop the knife."

"Hey, what's going on over there?" a man from the other side of the street asked. "I'm calling 911."

"Report a federal officer making an arrest needs backup!"

Her assailant backed away and glanced over his shoulder.

"Don't even think about it," she warned him, her forefinger trembling on the trigger.

"You won't shoot," he returned in a hoarse whisper and continued backing off. "You're still a virgin." With that, he fled.

Renata kept her weapon aimed, but he was weaving and there were people coming down the El steps and she wasn't a good enough shot to be sure of herself. She couldn't take a chance at missing her target and shooting an innocent bystander.

Besides, she *was* still a virgin—she'd never shot a living thing and she wasn't looking forward to losing that particular virginity.

She thought of going after her attacker, but he whipped up the El steps and she knew she would never catch him. He would hop on the next train and disappear. Ironic that some crazy person chose to attack an officer of the law.

"Are you all right?" the guy across the street shouted. "I made that call like you asked."

Hearing a siren in the distance, she said, "Thanks. Stick around—we'll need your name and number and your statement for the report."

"Uh, no thanks, don't have the time." The good citizen slinked into the night.

Blue light danced along the underpinnings of the rapid transit as a CPD squad barreled down Wabash and slowed as it approached her block. Slipping her gun back into the holster built into her purse, Renata stepped off the curb into the street and waved it down.

Normally, federal agencies handled their own investigations when an agent was involved in a violent crime, but this wasn't a normal situation, so she gave Officer Jules Jackson the report.

"The assailant was about six feet in height, medium build, wearing black jeans and a hoodie. The hood was pulled up. His face was dark, but I think he was wearing makeup," she said, examining the heel of her hand where she'd made contact. Something dark had rubbed off on her skin. "Some kind of camouflage." Renata gave him all the details of the attack itself as she remembered them. "Just before he ran," she concluded, "he said I wouldn't shoot because I was a virgin."

"Sounds like he knows you. How would he know you'd never shot anyone before?"

"Most people who own guns *don't* shoot other people." But she'd wondered, too.

"Don't you think it's a little odd that a stranger picked you out by chance to knife to death? You're sure you haven't ticked off someone lately?" he prodded, his dark face intent. "Maybe some scumbag you've been investigating on one of your cases?"

Thinking of the brouhaha in the media, she said, "Not anyone who would want to see me dead. At least I hope not."

But once she considered the possibility, the sharp talons of suspicion grabbed her and wouldn't let go.

Exhausted, Renata finished giving her statement, got a copy of the report and bade Officer Jackson a good night. Once in her apartment, she realized she was too wired to eat or sleep and began replaying the incident in her mind. She couldn't believe the assailant had caught her so off guard.

Of course, she'd never been attacked before…

A virgin…

How *had* he known?

So what if her attacker knew her or of her…why did he want her dead?

Only one thought came to her.

RENATA TESTED her new theory first thing the next morning, after sneaking into the S.A.F.E. offices via the loading dock door off the alley to avoid more reporters.

"The attack convinces me I was right about Hawass," she told her boss. "The only thing that makes sense is that the real shooter or one of his associates is trying to make sure I don't dig deeper."

"Your paranoia knows no bounds, Fox."

Ensconced behind his desk, his expression a combination of disbelief and disgust, Director Elliott Mulvihill stared at her through designer silver-rimmed glasses that complemented a gray designer suit. The director was probably only in his mid-fifties, but too much responsibility and early loss of hair—he was already half-bald—made him appear ten years older, despite the trendy ware. Or maybe his first wife and kids leaving him because of the job had done it. Or so went office gossip.

"Or is this a ploy...?" he asked. "This supposed attack."

"I have the police report. Would you like to see it?"

"Does it contain names and numbers of witnesses?"

Renata gaped at him.

"I thought not," he muttered, sounding satisfied.

Did he really believe she'd made up the whole thing?

Would he use the incident against her instead of protecting her? The only witness had scurried away. Even so, she hadn't thought she would lack support at her own agency.

This is what came from bucking the system.

"I suppose you have reason to believe you're

under attack," Mulvihill said. "So my advice to you is watch your back." He rose and from the end of his desk lifted a fat stack of loose papers which he held out to her. "In the meantime, I have myriad reports of possible terrorist threats I need analyzed. You're the perfect person for the job."

Knowing her blowing the whistle on him had prompted the extraordinary number of cases as punishment—perhaps the first of many—she chose to take the work from him without comment.

Trading his office for her cubicle, Renata wondered if she told her fellow agents what had happened to her last night, would they believe her? Or care? Or would they, too, dismiss her with a cold warning to watch her own back?

A co-worker was waiting for her in her cubicle—Thomas Alan Garvey, otherwise known as Tag, was sitting on her desk. The tall, lanky man with the hands of a master craftsman was the best shot on the S.A.F.E. sniper team and had been one of the men whose bullets had taken Hawass down.

"Good morning," she said optimistically.

"What the hell is good about it?" Tag demanded, his buzz cut seeming to bristle. "Unless you mean you really screwed your colleagues over good."

"I'm only trying to get to the truth, Tag. And to protect the citizens of this city," she added. "That doesn't mean I'm accusing anyone of anything but being led down the wrong path. And if Hawass wasn't the City Sniper, the shooter is still out there."

"Hawass was the sniper. What do you think was

in that package? *The* rifle," he said. "The labs came back positive. But that makes no nevermind for those of us who were in the trenches that day. The media won't leave us alone. And that means Internal Affairs is gonna get involved."

Renata tried to wrap her mind around this. "The labs were positive?"

"Hawass probably went for the rifle so he could set up his next target."

"Or he was set up—"

"Convince yourself of that if you can," Tag said, launching himself off her desk and out into the bull-pen.

Renata stared after the agency's top sharpshooter for a long few seconds before she took her seat behind her desk. Somehow she hadn't expected the rifle Hawass was carrying to be the one used to kill those five people. No wonder no one wanted to listen to her.

Even she started to second-guess herself…but no…she knew what she knew.

GABE WAITED until halfway through the day for Renata to call, hoping against hope that he'd gotten to his only link to Mulvihill.

When it became apparent that she wasn't going to call, he decided he would do the honors. Two rings and she picked up.

"Fox here."

Her honeyed voice sent a thrill through him that Gabe tried to ignore. "Agent Fox. Gabe Connor here."

Silence.

He waited it out.

Finally, she said, "What is it you want?"

"To help you. I told you that last night."

The honeyed voice became stiff with impatience. "And I told you I don't believe you."

"Why don't we get together to talk about it?"

"I don't need to get together. I've made up my mind. This is agency business."

"Then I'll have to work alone."

"What?"

"I mean, it would be more effective if we worked together, but—"

"You're a civilian!" Her voice was rich with indignation. "Stay out of this. You could get hurt!"

"Worried about me?" Gabe asked. "I'm flattered."

"Don't be. It's nothing personal. I would be worried about anyone who seemed crazy enough to go off on his own and get himself into trouble."

"Who says I'll get into trouble?"

"Look, Mr. Connor—"

"Gabe," he reminded her.

"I will handle this investigation. Go do whatever it is you do—"

"Security."

"Right. Security. Do that and leave the City Sniper investigation to me."

With that, she slammed down the phone, making Gabe jump.

Frustrated, he wondered what exactly he was going to have to do to wear her down enough to let him in.

NEEDING TO FEEL as if she were accomplishing something and wanting to put Gabriel Connor out of mind, Renata got to work on the reports Mulvihill had given her, reading and sorting them into three piles—probables, possibles and way out there.

She'd barely gotten started when the telephone rang.

Thinking it might be Gabe again—if not another reporter—she tersely answered, "Fox here."

"Agent Fox...Detective Stella Jacobek, Chicago Police Department. I have the report Officer Jackson made out last night and I would like to ask you some questions."

Great. Just what she needed after her go-round with Director Mulvihill—further involving the local police. The political ramifications stank.

"Listen, Detective, I haven't thought of anything I didn't tell the officer last night."

"I'm not worried about the details of the report being correct. I'm looking for motive."

"It wasn't robbery."

"I got that. Officer Jackson indicated the suspect probably knew you."

"It seems that way," Renata admitted. "But I honestly don't have a clue."

"If we work together on this—"

"That's not feasible and you know it."

She couldn't imagine what Mulvihill would do if she shared her suspicions with the detective. Federal agencies did cooperate on task forces like the one set up to tag the sniper, but not in this.

Detective Stella Jacobek apparently had some

similar ideas of her own when she said, "Considering your circumstances after the City Sniper—"

"Look, Detective, why don't you give me your number and if I think of anything, I'll call you."

Renata heard the sound of frustration come from the other woman, but she had the good sense to know when to give in. Unlike some people, namely Gabe Connor. The detective gave Renata her number, then said she would be calling her again after Renata had had time to think about why someone would want her dead.

As if she hadn't already thought about it.

Hanging up, Renata stared at the reports on her desk as if they were printed in a foreign language.

Concentrate, she ordered herself.

Not that she could just switch gears so easily. She had to force herself to pay attention because her mind naturally kept wandering back to the attack.

What if the sniper feared she'd stumbled onto some truth he wanted left buried? A truth worth killing her over. Her pulse ticking, Renata knew she wouldn't be safe until he was caught. But how was that supposed to happen?

No one at S.A.F.E. believed her report.

Mulvihill didn't even believe she'd been attacked.

So no one would be assigned to help her catch the real sniper.

Involving Detective Jacobek or anyone else from the CPD would be career suicide for her.

Which meant she'd have to do it herself.

Renata swallowed hard. She was the newest hire

in the Chicago office. She'd never so much as participated in a confrontation with offenders, let alone a fight for her life. Since being assigned, she'd done some investigation via phone or legwork, had drawn up a few profiles and had been responsible for a lot of paperwork.

Nothing had prepared her for this.

I'm available to take care of all your needs...

Heat filled Renata's cheeks as she remembered Gabe Connor's offer. Giving up the pretense of working, she dug into her shoulder bag and searched for his business card.

That didn't mean she trusted him. His showing up when he had...well, it raised alarms. Like...was he part of the solution...or part of the problem?

She found the card and stared at it.

Gabriel Connor...Chief of Security...Club Undercover.

Club telephone, cell, fax and address were listed across the bottom. But though Renata wanted to call him, suspicion made her hesitate. Too easy. He had some agenda.

But what?

Renata set the card away from her and went back to work. But every few paragraphs that she read, she glanced up to see the card sitting there, challenging her just as Gabe had.

Maybe she ought to check Gabe Connor out closer, see if his help might be the solution to her problem.

Chapter Three

Renata couldn't forget about Gabriel Connor. But as much as she wanted help from somewhere, it wasn't going to be from him.

She decided to tell him that in person and make sure he got the message. And maybe she could figure out him and his agenda while she was at it.

Meeting with him in person would charge up the instincts she'd developed while getting an advanced degree in psychology and working as a mediator. After all, her experience analyzing people and their motivations, their strengths and their weaknesses, had been the deciding factor in S.A.F.E.'s hiring her. Before she gave up, she was going to use her own abilities to help herself out of this jam.

Alighting from a taxi, she noted the crowd lined up outside of an older building with a pale green tile facade and a large neon sign announcing it as Club Undercover. A glance down Milwaukee Avenue revealed the city skyline a few miles southeast. Its proximity to downtown and good transportation made the Wicker Park/Bucktown neighborhood increasingly popular with an eclectic mix, both to live and to be entertained.

Waiting to get into the club, hip-hop, street-wear-clad Gen-Yers were shoulder-to-shoulder with alternative, grunge Gen-Xers and Armani-dressed yuppies. Unusual hair colors, tattoos and body piercings were tested alongside designer everything.

Feeling out of the loop wearing a simple dress beneath her coat, Renata got into the line, which moved quickly down a wide flight of stairs toward the lower-level entrance. But suddenly movement stopped.

"There's a wait for tables," a woman with dark hair streaked a deep blue announced over a dissatisfied rumble. "Bar space only."

Exactly what she'd planned to do—sit at the bar, get a feel for the place and see what she could learn about the club's head of security.

Entering the dark cave decorated in blue-and-red neon, Renata squeezed her eardrums against the music that blasted her. How did anyone talk over this noise? Feeling less confident about getting that information she wanted, she nevertheless checked her coat, then circled the dance floor crowded with gyrating bodies and made it to the bar.

"What can I get you?" asked the bartender.

"Shiraz," she said, not sure if he'd heard her.

But he nodded and went to get her drink. Maybe he read lips, she thought wryly, noting how he stuck out in the polished place. Tall and broad-shouldered, he wore a soft brown shirt and a leather pouch hanging from his neck. His hair was dark and long, secured in back with strips of leather. When he set the drink in front of her, she took a better look at his face and realized they had something in common. He, too, was part Native American.

And as if on cue, the music segued to something smoother and softer.

"Good crowd," she said. "Is it like this every night?"

"Worse on weekends," he returned. "Or even better in the management's point of view."

"Crowd control must be a challenge."

"We have good security. Bouncers."

Checking the room and spotting them easily—they were a little too alert, a little too stiff to be customers—she prompted, "And security officers?"

"You could call them that. I get the impression you have an interest."

So he'd read right through her. She might as well be direct. "What do you think of your head of security?"

"Gabriel Connor? He's a good man." The bartender's gaze shifted over her shoulder. "But you can check him out for yourself."

Renata swivelled on her stool and banged her knees right into the man who'd come up behind her.

"Agent Fox, what a pleasant surprise."

Was it really? From his self-satisfied expression, she would guess he'd been expecting her.

"You aroused my curiosity," she admitted.

"Well, that's a start."

Despite her determination to view the encounter as a piece of necessary business, Renata felt herself flush. She also found herself concentrating on his mouth, both sensual and generous with a smile.

That mouth said, "Let's go someplace where we can talk," and her response became instantly physical—a fluttering deep down in her belly.

"All right."

When Gabe took her glass of wine, their fingers brushed and she fought a case of nerves that followed her all the way up a flight of stairs opposite the dance floor. This seemed to be a VIP lounge if the patrons were any indication. Rather than wild hair and tattoos, elegant women wore jewels. She recognized a city politician and a news anchorman and a local entertainer. It seemed Club Undercover was the hot spot du jour.

Renata realized it was quieter up on this level, as well. No speakers blaring at them. But Gabe didn't stop at one of the velvet-upholstered booths.

He took her around the bar into a back room that combined storage—boxes of wine and beer were stacked along one wall—and security by way of an equipment rack. Three monitors covered the VIP area and VCRs recorded the activity. And before them sat a young guy who looked like he could take care of himself.

"Reese."

The young security guard jumped to his feet. "Mr. Connor."

"I told you to call me Gabe. Take twenty. Actually, make sure we're done in here before you disturb us."

"Yes, sir."

Renata felt Reese's eyes on her as he circled them and slipped into the lounge.

Gabe indicated she should sit on one of the wheeled chairs before the monitors. When Renata slid into it, he took the other and his knee brushed hers before he rolled back a bit. Her nerves flared at the brief contact and she felt herself flush with warmth.

"So you wanted to check me out first," Gabe mused, handing the wine back to her.

Avoiding his fingers, Renata took the glass, asking, "Do you blame me?"

"I've been told I'm not too hard on the eyes and that I have my moments of charm."

Trying to ignore those very facts—he was playing her and she knew it—Renata said, "You know that's not what I meant." She didn't want to notice how good he looked, his dark green silk shirt not only intensifying the green of his eyes but also doing nothing to hide the musculature it covered.

"Too bad," he said wistfully. "It's business, then."

"I still want to know your interest."

"*You* interest me."

Gabe's voice was so mellow it made her toes curl. Annoyed, Renata steeled herself and said, "You can stop being charming now."

"I didn't know I'd started."

"If this is as serious as you get, maybe I've made a mistake coming here."

She moved to leave, but as he had the night before, Gabe stopped her. Once more, his hand on her arm was strong without being cruel. Still, she could feel each finger imprinted on her flesh...

"I told you never to touch me—"

"How serious do you want me to be?" he interrupted. And then let go.

Was he trying to distract her? Why? Warmth flooded her. If she made a big deal of it now, she would only get farther from her objective.

Renata forced herself to concentrate. "I want you to tell me why you tracked me down."

"I did tell you—"

"This time, tell me the truth."

Gabe's expression darkened and she could see the war within him. He didn't want to talk. But if he didn't, how could she trust him?

As if realizing his silence would be a deal-breaker, he said, "Someone I cared about was in the wrong place at the wrong time and was killed for no other reason."

"I'm sorry."

His forehead pulled in a frown and tension oozed from Gabe like a palpable thing, and Renata realized he was waiting for her to press him. She wanted more, but she knew she wasn't going to get it.

"All right, so it's personal," she said. "Now how did you find me?"

His forehead lost that washboard look as he relaxed. "That was easy. I let my fingers do the walking. S.A.F.E.'s address is in the phone book."

"But how did you know I would be there?"

"I called the office."

"No one told me I had a call or message."

"I didn't ask them to."

"And how did you know what time I was going to leave?" she asked.

"I didn't. I waited outside, and for a couple of hours, I might add. You probably work days that are far too long. A type A plus personality." When she opened her mouth to protest, he continued, "And before you ask how I knew what you looked like, your photo was front-page news."

"I wasn't going to ask that."

"Then what?"

"Why last night?"

"Why not? The story was in yesterday morning's paper. Should I have waited?"

Wanting to know for certain whether or not he'd somehow set her up for the attack, Renata watched his face closely as she said, "Someone else was waiting for me last night outside my apartment building. *He* had a knife."

Silence fell between them and she could see a flicker of shock in Gabe's eyes and something more cross his features. He hadn't known, then. Realizing she'd been holding her breath, Renata let it out.

"At least you're not hurt. I mean you look okay."

"I am…other than my boss not believing me…" For the first time since she'd put her report together,

Renata thought maybe someone was on her side. It was a good feeling, even if she couldn't take his help. But she still wanted to know whatever it was Gabe knew. Maybe *that* would help her. "What is it you think you can do for me that I can't do for myself?"

"Give you a fresh eye, for one. Someone to bounce ideas off of. I can't imagine any of your colleagues is in the right frame of mind for that."

"No, not right now." Even Paul Broden, as supportive of her as he was personally, didn't believe her conclusions. "What else?"

"Isn't that enough? What did you expect—that I would have the answers?"

Gabe was grinning at her again and Renata shifted in her chair. She wished he would stop that—disarming her at every turn. He flustered her, made her lose her train of thought. It took some doing to recoup her concentration.

"Look, I'm the new agent in the Chicago office, and if I screw this case up…"

"So we won't screw up."

"We…that's the other thing. If Elliott Mulvihill found out I was working with an outsider, he would crucify my career."

"I won't tell. How about you?"

"There are other ways he can find out."

"That's a risk you'll just have to take."

"But are you worth it?"

He sat back and stared at her. "That's something only you can answer."

Gabe Connor was definitely a wild card.

"I'm sorry," she said. "But you're still a civilian. I can't use you."

What passed for a smile softened his rough beard-stubbled features, giving her another glimpse of that charm. There was something of the con man about Gabe and Renata wondered about his background.

Trusting him was out of the question.

Chapter Four

Gabe could tell Renata didn't trust him, that he had a ways to go to convince her to go along with his program. Talk about someone *he* shouldn't trust... she was a government agent. Not that he meant her any harm. On the contrary, he hoped his involvement in her investigation would do her some good.

And maybe he would get the answers he needed.

He automatically checked the monitors to make certain no one was paying too much attention to the storeroom doors. Maybe he should have brought Renata into the main security office downstairs, but he figured they had less chance of being interrupted or overheard up here. He hadn't wanted one of the other members of Team Undercover to preempt him before he heard the facts and manufactured a plan of some kind.

"Just out of curiosity, if I had said yes, how much would your help have cost me?" Renata asked, a touch of cynicism in her voice.

"I'm not for hire," he said, relaxing, making sure

not one set of eyes was aimed their way before moving his gaze to her. "Think of me as a volunteer."

"No one does anything for nothing."

He couldn't deny that. Neither could he tell her what he hoped to gain. If he did, she would stop him. Anyone working for the government seemed to think that was his or her right. Or so experience had taught him.

"Maybe I simply have too much free time on my hands," he said, letting his lips curl into a crooked smile. He lifted one eyebrow and gave her a heated look. "Or maybe I simply want to impress you."

She raised both eyebrows, seemingly unimpressed. "You don't know me."

"But I plan to."

Renata blinked and seemed to be trying to hide her thoughts on that one. Gabe always knew when a woman was interested in him, and he had no doubt this one was.

The idea of something developing between them beyond the investigation set his own hormones racing. Eyes dark and smoky, lips well-defined with bright red, Renata was stunning tonight. Her lush dark hair fell like a silky cloud around her, but that was no body of an angel. Encased in simple black, every curve tempted him.

Preferring to hold the reins and keep control, he shifted away from her and said, "Let's say I accept your refusal to let me help you. Can I just ask about your involvement in the case? That should be a matter of public record, right?"

She blinked again. "I'll have to go some to be on

the same wavelength with you." But she pulled herself together fast enough. "Telling you won't hurt anything, I guess. Director Mulvihill asked me to look at all the facts of the case to see if I could come up with some kind of profile on the shooter. Maybe stop him from killing again."

"You're trained to do that?"

"Not by the FBI. Not formally. But I am trained to know people and how their minds work. I was a corporate mediator and had to be able to read people to do my job."

"But that's on a one-to-one basis. In the City Sniper case, you only had paperwork to go on, right?"

She nodded. "That's mostly how it works anyway. Unfortunately, the lack of pattern threw me at first, but eventually I realized that each of the victims had something in his or her past that took him or her off the straight and narrow. Some more than others. But you already know that from the media coverage. While everyone believed the shootings were random, I found that link that told me otherwise."

"Which you thought would go where?"

"I'm not sure."

"But you have a theory." From her expression, Gabe could see that she had.

"I wondered if they could all have been in on some plan together," she admitted. "I don't know what—a robbery, or maybe a con job. Maybe they had information that threatened the shooter. Maybe they were planning a crime together and turned on him. Or they could have committed a crime as a team and the shooter was covering his back by getting rid of his partners…and therefore witnesses. I simply didn't have enough to go on."

"So you told Mulvihill about the connection when?"

"As they were rolling out after Hawass. I tried to stop the operation, but it's impossible to stop a witch-hunt in progress when you don't have any power."

"You gave your boss the report?"

"Later. Mulvihill didn't even stop to consider my theory…then when I did turn in the written report the next day, he buried it. His reasoning was that, unless there actually was a sniping incident, he was going to assume they got the right target. He didn't want the kind of bad press S.A.F.E. got after Embry Lake last spring."

Gabe cursed softly. The sniper fiasco fit Mulvihill to a *T*—he was a man too eager to pounce on his prey to listen to reason. If nothing else, someone had to stop the director of S.A.F.E. from doing more harm, and that someone was going to be him. He'd been looking for a way to get to the man and now this opportunity had fallen in his lap.

He wasn't going to pass that up.

"I might not have done anything," Renata admitted, "but then Hawass's sister gave her brother an alibi for one of the shootings."

"I didn't hear about that."

"I wonder why. And she claims the day her

brother was shot, he had no intention of leaving the house until after he received a phone call."

"From whom?"

"She didn't know. He up and left without an explanation."

"And Mulvihill knew to go after him how?"

"Another phone call," Renata said. "From a reliable informant. And since Hawass was already under watch, Mulvihill jumped at the chance to get him."

"Sounds like a setup."

"Someone who wanted Muti Hawass out of the way," she agreed. "I wondered if the caller realized he would be ruining the Hawass family, as well."

Gabe could see that fact concerned her. "So what about the victims?"

"This was all covered in the news reports."

"Indulge me."

"I'm not going to tell you anything you couldn't get with a little digging."

Yes, she would, whether she thought so or not, Gabe thought. But all he said was "So?"

She frowned at him, tried to stall him, but he could see she needed someone to talk to.

"The struggling actress, Mae Chin—she's also been a personal escort."

"So you think she's a high-priced hooker."

Renata shrugged. "We don't have proof of that, but that's a fair assumption. Then there's Maurice Washington, the owner of a club on the South Side—he's suspected of selling Ecstasy at his club."

"Any arrests?"

"Yes, but no convictions. The only sniper victim actually convicted of anything was Chuck LaRoe, a clerk in an independent bookstore, but he was simply part of an anti-war protest without a permit."

"But he wasn't incarcerated."

"No. He got a stern lecture and probation. He's lucky they didn't try him under the Patriot Act."

Gabe thought about the victims. There could have been a link between a hooker and drug dealer. But a peacenik? That didn't compute.

There had been five victims, so he asked, "So what about the other two?"

"Heidi Bourne, aide to U.S. Congressman Carl Cooper, was caught in a government scandal, but she made a deal and was going to testify against her boss. And Gary Hudson, a divorce lawyer, was arrested for domestic violence. His wife thought twice and dropped the charges."

The last stuck in Gabe's craw.

How many times had his abused mother cut his father some slack until one day he almost killed her?

It was only then, with her stuck in a hospital bed, that Gabe had convinced his mother that it was time to leave the bastard and disappear forever. Even then, she'd been afraid to do it, but he'd told her that if his father laid a hand on her or him or his kid brother one more time, he would kill the man himself and let the law do with him what it would. Gabe had been thirteen at the time, his brother Danny only eight.

His mother had realized Gabe was serious when

he detailed how he would kill his own father. Which gun he would use. What kind of ammunition.

After all, he'd been bred to it...

Fearing for her sons, if not for herself, his mother had taken them and fled the day before she was to be released from the hospital. But once on the run, the running never seemed to stop. The fear that his father would catch up to them had always hung over their heads.

The fear that he would become his father hung over his.

Realizing Renata was staring at him, her brow furrowed as if she were trying to read *him*, Gabe cleared his throat and asked, "But you didn't find any actual connection between the five victims, right?"

"I never had a chance to find out. It wasn't in the case files."

"Can you get me a copy of your report?"

"Excuse me? If you'll remember, I refused your help."

"But you're still talking to me."

"I guess that was a mistake," Renata said. "Coming here to tell you no in person was a mistake."

"The mistake was your saying no. You need me."

"No, I really don't."

"Even if your life is on the line?"

He heard her quick intake of breath before she recovered. Was she afraid of seeming too vulnerable?

She might read people for a living, but reading people was part of his life experience. He'd gotten good at it from the time he was a kid, gotten better as an adult. If he hadn't, he might not be alive today. She was torn. She wanted his help even if she hadn't yet accepted it.

"We'll get him, whoever he is," Gabe promised Renata. "It'll be a career-maker."

"Or breaker."

"Not if you succeed," he said.

"Seeing justice done is reward enough for me."

"I stopped believing in justice long ago."

"Maybe when I nail the guilty one, I'll turn you into a believer."

For a government agent, Renata Fox really was naive, though Gabe counted it as one of her many charms. Then again, if Mulvihill went down, she just might succeed in turning him around.

Renata said, "This is my case. You have nothing to do with it, do you understand? I'm going to work alone and find the real sniper before he can score another victim."

As in her, Gabe added silently, not wanting to see anything happen to this woman.

When she rose as if to go, he said, "Wait. One more thing. Tell me what happened last night. I swear I know nothing about it."

She looked at him closely when she said, "I was on my block when someone rushed me from behind—a guy wearing a hoodie and camouflage that hid his identity. And, oh, yeah, he was carrying a big knife."

Gabe's gut tightened on the word *knife*. The attacker *had* meant to kill her.

She went on. "We struggled, and I pulled my weapon and got a drop on the bastard, who then booked on me."

Either she was very, very good or very, very lucky. "Then he didn't believe you would shoot him."

"He seemed to be convinced of that."

Which convinced Gabe of Renata's vulnerability and of her need for support from him and Gideon and the others. Using her to get the dirt on someone was one thing. But he didn't want to be responsible for someone else's life in the process.

"Let's head back downstairs," he suggested, wondering how he could talk her into a Team Undercover mood. "Reese's twenty minutes are up."

Beating her to the door, he held it open. Indeed, his security guard was cooling his heels at the bar. Gabe signaled him and Reese nodded and headed back to VIP control central, such as it was, for the rest of the shift.

Renata set her half-filled glass of wine on the bar before leading the way across the lounge. Gabe couldn't help but admire the sway of her hips, clad close in a sexy black dress. When they got to the stairs, he lightly touched the back of her waist as they descended. Either she was too preoccupied to notice his hand on her again or she chose to ignore the fact.

He leaned into her and got a whiff of her scent, exotic and spicy, and it took effort to remember what he wanted to say. Oh, yeah...

"It doesn't have to be just me," he said. "I can always bring in reinforcements to speed up the process, get this over quicker."

"No! No one else. Not even you. I work alone."

He ignored her protest, saying, "The bartender you were interrogating earlier, for instance—Blade Stone—he was Special Ops."

And had been a major participant in one of Team Undercover's cases when Gabe had arrived at the club. He'd saved a woman from being killed by her stalker.

"No one!" she insisted.

Damn! She was going to make his mission more difficult than it needed to be, not to mention the protection angle. Just thinking about finding her stabbed to death made his gut knot. Why couldn't she simply take a chance on him?

He guessed he didn't blame her, though. Hell, considering the way he'd been playing her, he didn't blame Renata for being suspicious and cautious—he wouldn't trust him, either. Hopefully, once he wore her down and she agreed to his help and they started working together, she would loosen up and give him the benefit of the doubt.

Then he could bring in the others.

If she thought she could make him give up and go away, then…well, she simply didn't know him.

As they neared the dance floor, Gabe spotted Gideon at the club entrance, looking around, probably for him. Gideon knew Renata was here and would assume he'd sold the Team Undercover package to her.

Knowing he needed to keep Renata away from the boss—and the others—at least for now, Gabe said, "Let's dance."

And even though getting this close was insanity, he swung Renata fully into his arms and onto the dance floor.

SHE WAS TRAPPED. Gabe Connor had gone and wrapped her in his arms on a dance floor, where she could do nothing to free herself without making a scene.

"Were you always a rebel?" Renata asked tightly. "When you were a kid, I mean. Did you always do things people told you not to do?"

"Always. Revolutions make life worth living."

Which meant he hadn't given up, even if his statement sounded more ironic than serious, Renata thought. As if that was the last thing in the world he really believed.

What did he believe in? she wondered. *What made Gabe Connor tick?*

At the moment, he was making *her* tick.

Renata inched her hips away from his slightly, but there was no getting away from the man, not really. Their fit seemed custom-made, and Gabe surrounded her with himself in a way she couldn't resist. A grand tease, that's what this was. Enough to make her yearn for more, to get even closer, even though she knew Gabriel Connor was the last man on earth she should involve herself with personally.

She would have to be careful…not let this happen again…but for now…for this one crazy moment, she would allow herself to get lost in the music and the closeness and the fancy footwork.

"Someone taught you to make all the right moves," she said, as his thighs brushed hers, the sensual contact nearly making her lose her breath.

"Actually, I make them up as I go along."

He demonstrated, doing a twisty-turny thing that made her laugh.

"Nice sound," he said then. "Practice it much?"

"Not lately," she admitted.

"We'll have to fix that."

He synched his movements to the end of the piece so they finished in an exaggerated dip, their position that of two lovers. The noisy room faded in an instant and Renata imagined Gabe was about to seduce her.

Then he let her up and scanned the room as if he were looking for someone.

Uneasy now, she asked, "Lose something?" and looked, too.

Then Gabe focused totally on her again and patted the spot over his heart. "Only inside."

Despite the fact that she knew he was joking, Renata felt her own chest squeeze a little tighter. This flirtation thing was getting to be too much for her.

"Let's get out of here," he said.

"I'm getting out. You have a job here."

"Which I'm trying to do. I'm seeing to a patron's safety by escorting her home."

"That won't be necessary." His seeing her home would be a mistake with her in this crazy mood.

"I disagree. With me along, there won't be a repeat of last night. To that point, you probably should find some temporary digs."

Feeling as if his company were inevitable no matter what her protest, Renata stopped at the check station to get her coat. "I won't be driven out of my home."

"How about carried?"

"You're a real comedian."

"That's what I've been told."

"Don't let it go to your head."

The smart retort relieved some of the physical tension between them and by the time they got into his car, Renata was actually able to relax. She wondered how she should justify letting him drive her home, though.

Not knowing what else to do to distract herself, Renata fetched her cell phone and checked to see if anyone had called. Someone had. She made out the number. Her mom again. Great. Well, she would have to wait until she got home to return the call. She certainly didn't want Gabe to be party to that particular conversation.

Her mom would bring up what had happened to her dad—how his death had been a result of all the pressure—and she would then have to reassure Mom that the same thing wouldn't happen to her. Would her mother ever get over her loss and get on with her life? Renata wondered. Maybe meet a new man? The kind of love her mom had for her dad was downright scary—Mom simply couldn't let go.

Renata was never going to let that happen to her.

She was also a stickler for details and wouldn't let go of anything vaguely suspicious, so she would be okay. Even so, she suddenly got a visual of the guy with the knife and had to shut the attack from her mind.

"Do you really have to know the second you get a call?" Gabe asked.

Realizing she was still hanging on to the phone, she said, "In my line of work, any call might be important."

"I get the feeling it's more than your work. It's a reflection of your personality."

A criticism? "Like what?"

"Are we a little obsessive-compulsive?"

"Don't try to analyze me!" she snapped. "Psychoanalyzing people is *my* field, remember? And I suppose you never check your messages."

"I don't own a cell phone."

Which Renata found hard to believe. "Why not?" She couldn't help herself. "Paranoid that someone will triangulate your signal to track you down?"

He glanced at her and grinned. "Hey, you made a joke."

"Obsessive-compulsive people can occasionally enjoy humor," she informed him.

"I'll remember that. And about the cell phone…I don't want to be reached wherever I am. I like my privacy."

"What about emergencies? And if you want privacy, you can shut the phone off."

"So why don't you?"

Seeing this wasn't an argument either of them was going to win, Renata chose to keep her obsessive-compulsive mouth shut until they arrived outside of her place and he double-parked the car.

Hand on the door handle, she said, "I appreciate your offer of help, Gabe." Even though she still didn't know why he'd made it. "And I'm sorry that I can't take it."

"You don't sound sorry."

"All right. So I was trying to be polite." She started to leave the car.

"Whoa, I'll see you to your door."

"Stay where you are! This isn't a date," she protested, ignoring the part of her that almost wished it was.

"Maybe not with me, but what about with Mr. Hoodie?"

The reference shot her pulse up even further, and she searched the area for any trace of her attacker, even as she opened the door, saying, "I can take care of myself like I *did* take care of myself last night."

She didn't need alone time with Gabe, not after the way she'd responded to him on the dance floor. She needed to focus on her work. On this case. She needed to succeed, to allow her family to regain its pride.

Luckily, no one was waiting for her tonight.

So she slid out of the car and headed straight for her doorway. The driver's door opened and as she keyed in her code to get inside, she glanced over her shoulder to see if Gabe had followed.

He hadn't moved away from the car.

Even so…somehow it made her feel better that he had her back.

Chapter Five

The next morning, Gabe started his own investigation without Renata. He did some computer tracking and got a little more information on the victims, but not enough to think it was worth his while. This was going to take some old-fashioned legwork. He decided to begin by seeing what he could find out about victim number two, Maurice Washington, whose club, Get the Blues, was located in a South Side neighborhood that had seen better days.

On his way there, he thought about Renata. She wouldn't agree to his help. She didn't trust him; how could he blame her, when he'd hidden his own agenda? He didn't like the way it made him feel, especially when he was around her. He didn't like using people—he'd been on the other end of that stick and it sucked.

Even though she was a government agent and therefore worthy of his own suspicions, Gabe realized his half-truths and evasions bothered him more than he liked to admit. He was attracted to Renata and wouldn't mind knowing her more intimately. But more importantly, he both liked and respected the woman. She was as straight-arrow as they came. No matter the cost to herself, she put herself on the line when she saw injustice. You couldn't ask for more than that of anyone.

And that's why he was getting himself involved, with or without her permission. In the hope that justice really could be done. He had to remember his purpose was the most important factor here. He wasn't doing this for himself. He was doing this for Danny. And for Muti Hawass and his family. And for any future victims of Elliott Mulvihill.

It was early afternoon when he parked his car at a meter across from Get the Blues and next to a mural that covered the entire side of the building. The Blues Wall, as it was called, chronicled the birth and growth of the blues and the historic struggle of black musicians for acceptance in a segregated society. The protest mural made a powerful statement in a neighborhood that had no power but that of the streets.

A couple of guys in their late teens or early twenties seemed to appear out of nowhere, as if checking on Gabe's intentions. Nodding politely to them, Gabe crossed to check out the club.

It wasn't open, of course. Too early. But a sign indicated it would be open that night for business, featuring a local performer whose name he didn't recognize. Someone was still keeping the joint alive.

A someone he wanted to meet.

Gabe turned and met the two who'd followed him with a head-on stare. "Either of you guys know who's running the club these days? I'm looking for information. I'm following up on Maurice Washington's murder. I'm not a cop," he assured them. "This is a private matter."

The two looked him over and conferred in tones so hushed he couldn't hear.

One of them said, "Then you gotta talk to the man in charge of the wall. Right, Odell?"

"Who might that be?" Gabe asked.

"Aaron Brown," Odell said. "I'll take you to him. De-Ron, watch his car."

De-Ron said, "Okay. That'll be ten dead presidents."

Knowing it was the politic thing to do, Gabe tipped De-Ron ten bucks before following Odell back to the muraled wall and what looked like a shuttered convenience store. The owner came to the door, looking as if he'd been awakened.

Odell said something and pointed and Gabe noted Brown gave him a once-over before nodding.

Odell sauntered back to Gabe. "Says you can go on in, that he's open for business now."

Which made it sound like Gabe was going to have to pay for any information. So upon entering the poorly lit store that he figured was a front for some other kind of business, Gabe grabbed a flashlight and set it down on the counter.

"How much?"

If the owner of the store had been sleeping, he was

wide awake now. Strange pale gray eyes in a freck-led café-au-lait face gave him a thorough once over.

"That'll be fifty."

Gabe knew the man didn't mean cents. He pulled out his wallet and passed the store owner a fifty-dollar bill, saying, "I understand you knew Maurice Washington. Did he have any enemies?"

Brown laughed, showing bright white teeth that looked newly bonded. "A man like Maurice always has enemies. But none of 'em can hit a target worth a damn. So if you're thinkin' one of 'em took him down…" The store owner shook his head.

"What about associates? Did you ever hear him mention Mae Chin?"

"That one of the women killed by the sniper?

"She was the first."

Again, Brown shook his head. "Maurice didn't know nothing about her or that lawyer. People 'round here were getting whacked by the second shooting. Maurice woulda told me if he knew either of 'em."

"How about a man named Elliott Mulvihill?"

"Never heard of him."

"Maybe you've seen him." Despite the laid-back attitude, Gabe would bet Brown saw a whole lot oth-ers didn't. "He's fiftyish, balding, wears glasses and designer suits."

"In this neighborhood? You gotta be kiddin'."

Gabe tried not to show his disappointment at not being able to make a direct connection. "So who's running Get the Blues now? And how can I find him?"

"Maurice had a silent partner, but he's not so silent any more." Aaron smiled. "You need some extra batteries for that flashlight, right?"

"Right." Gabe grabbed a pack and slapped it down on the counter, then pulled out another bill and set it next to his "purchases." "His name?"

"Aaron Brown, Esquire." Brown's grin widened, showing off his bonded teeth.

Gritting his, Gabe gave the man his card. "In case you think of anything else you want to sell me."

He left the store in disgust. A hundred bucks up in smoke. Make that a hundred and ten, he thought, reminded of De-Ron's tip when he saw the guy leaning against his car. Not a thing for his trouble or money.

He was just getting started, Gabe told himself. He couldn't expect to hit the jackpot on his first try.

"WHAT IS IT you think you're doing?" Renata asked Gabe.

He'd picked her up on a corner two blocks from her office. No way had she been willing to wait for him in front of the building where she knew that media types—while smaller in numbers—still waited to pounce on her. She was hoping they would fade into the woodwork if she could tap-dance around them long enough.

"I'm working the case," he said.

"I told you I couldn't accept your help."

"And I told you I was going to investigate on my own. What are you going to do about it? Arrest me?"

That's all she would need was to make more waves, get herself in front of the media yet again. But no matter what she said to deter him, Gabe was apparently set on defying her. He'd investigated Maurice Washington, had possibly alerted people she didn't want alerted.

Trapped by Gabe. Again. First on the dance floor, this time on the streets.

He was doing some dance with her now. He was a wild card. Better that she knew what he was up to…the only way she could control him…the only way she could protect him. Besides, if she didn't say yes, he would simply keep on and maybe ruin her case.

A no-win situation for her.

"All right," she said, trying to keep the resentment out of her voice. "As long as you promise me that you're not going to go off on your own again."

"So you want me to stick with you," he said, grinning.

"Promise," she said through gritted teeth.

"It's all I wanted from the first."

She noticed he didn't actually make that promise, though.

"So where does Mulvihill think you are?" Gabe asked before she could make an issue of it.

"The director wasn't around to question me, thankfully," Renata said. "I simply signed out and left."

Gabe asked, "Making your own hours won't get you into trouble?"

"I'm already in trouble. I want to be alive to see how this case all works out. Let's head for Chinatown. Mae Chin's mother is a hostess at Three Dragons."

Having trouble concentrating on the busy work Mulvihill had pushed on her, Renata had felt an unwanted bubble of excitement at hearing Gabe's voice…until he'd dropped the bomb on her that he'd already investigated Maurice Washington on his own. Without thinking it through, she'd insisted on seeing him in person so she could tell him to lay off.

This was her job, after all.

More importantly, this was her life.

But that didn't seem to matter to him. He was determined to keep his attractive nose where it didn't belong, no matter what she said.

Since Chinatown was one of the closest South Side neighborhoods, it took less than ten minutes to arrive. Gabe drove them right into the heart of the busy area, which was crowned by the green-roofed gate, one of the few Asian-looking structures.

Luckily, he found a parking spot on a side street just off Wentworth. So he fed the meter, while Renata peered into an herb shop window, fascinated by the products displayed, many of which were unavailable elsewhere in the city.

"Ready?" Gabe asked in a low voice, his lips so near her ear she could feel his breath.

Renata jumped inside, yet tried to keep a cool demeanor. No matter what her attraction, this was business. Serious business. Keeping that in mind, she strolled with him, looking for the peaked tile roof of the restaurant down the street.

"So what are you hoping to get from the mother that we didn't?" Renata asked. "Someone from our office already interviewed anyone we could find related to the victims."

"Did you find Aaron Brown?"

"Aaron Brown...name's not familiar."

"He was Maurice Washington's silent partner, but he's not so silent now."

"Oh."

How had they missed that? she wondered, trying to remember the report and who the investigating agents had talked to about the club owner, other than a couple of bartenders and waitresses and a lone brother who lived in a south suburb.

"Talking to Lian Chin is a place to start," Gabe said. "Besides, you wouldn't let me look at the files," he reminded her. "So I don't know who was already interviewed or what information they already gave."

"Nothing we were able to use to make a case," she said as they reached their destination.

The front of the restaurant was decorated by three pillars carved into dragons, hence the name. It was one of the remaining old "chop suey palaces" catering to American palates. Though Renata had heard of the restaurant, she'd never eaten there. And though she'd been a lifelong Chicago resident, she'd never even been to Chinatown before Mae Chin had been executed.

"Just let me do all the talking," Renata said, on edge when Gabe didn't respond.

The woman who greeted them at the door, menus in hand, wore a name tag that identified her as Lian. She was a tiny woman in aqua silk, her still-dark hair pulled back into a long braid. "Table for two?"

"Lian Chin? Agent Renata Fox with S.A.F.E." She showed the woman her identification. "This is Gabe Connor. We'd like to ask you a few questions about your daughter."

The woman's face crumpled as if she were going to cry, but she pulled it together and asked them to sit in an empty booth while she got someone to take over for her.

The interior was dimly lit and furnished with curved black upholstered booths on one wall and glass tables, with dragons for legs, in the center. A black vase, decorated with a red dragon and filled with exotic blooms, nestled in a corner.

When Mae's mother came back to the table and slid in next to Renata, Gabe said, "Mrs. Chin, I'm very sorry for your loss."

"Thank you. We can't bring her back, but at least they stopped the criminal who killed my daughter from killing anyone else."

"Maybe."

The woman's almond eyes rounded. "What are you saying?"

"What Gabe meant," Renata broke in smoothly, wishing he would be seen and not heard, "is that we're still trying to put the pieces together. We're trying to see if there were any connections between the victims."

"I already told you people everything I know. I never heard of the other victims before reading about them."

"Maybe your daughter knew them through her work," Gabe suggested before Renata could resume questioning.

Renata kicked him under the table and gave him a look.

"You think they might be connected with the theater or movie business?" Mrs. Chin asked.

"We don't mean her career as an actress," Renata said. "Her other job."

Mrs. Chin frowned. "What other job?"

"I'm sorry to be blunt, Mrs. Chin, but we think sometimes she acted as an escort for out-of-town businessmen," Gabe said smoothly. "When she wasn't in a play or movie."

Renata was ready to strangle him. She'd told him to let her do the talking and he was taking over the interview.

"Escort? Oh, no. My daughter concentrated on her acting career. I supported her choice, paid for her apartment and her acting lessons while she was auditioning and getting small roles in the theater. Then she started making those low-budget Asian action films. She was so talented and so beautiful—she could have been the next Lucy Liu if not for her manager."

"Her manager?" Renata echoed.

"Fred Woo. He always held her back."

"I don't remember any Fred Woo from the files,"

Renata said. "Did you talk to anyone about him before?"

"I must have." But the woman's expression grew puzzled as if she weren't sure. "For several months, I tried to get Mae to fire Woo and get herself a new manager. She kept saying she couldn't...but then she changed her mind." Mrs. Chin ducked her head. "Mae said she had something on Woo that would make him release her from her contract...only she waited too long." When she looked up, her eyes were swimming with unshed tears. "Maybe if she'd have made the break sooner, she would have been in L.A. on a movie set instead of the shopping center, and the sniper wouldn't have killed her."

Renata swallowed hard and gave the woman a minute.

It was Gabe who asked, "Are your daughter's possessions still in her apartment?"

The woman nodded. "I haven't been able to force myself to pack up her things. I keep expecting Mae to walk in the door and tell me it was all a big mistake and her action double was the one who really died."

Renata blinked in surprise when Gabe reached out and covered the woman's hand with his own and gave it a sympathetic squeeze. She knew what it was like to lose a loved one to violence—hard to accept, at times unbelievable and always haunting. She wondered if Gabe knew firsthand, as well. That he was being so kind to the woman touched her.

"Y-you want to see my daughter's apartment?" Mrs. Chin asked.

Gabe nodded and softly said, "If that would be okay with you."

Mae's apartment was on the next block. Her mother let them in and then asked they set the lock when they left, saying she couldn't bear to come inside herself. The apartment was small but colorful, swaths of bright cloth hanging from the windows and covering the second-hand chairs and couch.

As they began their search, Renata said, "When I told you to let me do the talking, which part of that order didn't you understand?"

"Order? You don't give orders to your partner."

"You're not my partner!" she said, exasperated.

"Then what am I doing here?"

"I've been wondering that myself. I'm tempted to take you somewhere and handcuff you so you can't—"

"Handcuffs?" he interrupted. "Kinky. But I'm flexible, willing to try new things."

Wanting to scream, Renata swallowed it and got to work.

But a search of the living room and the bedroom gave them nothing new other than manager Fred Woo's phone number, which Renata found stamped on the back of a glossy photo of the young woman, the kind of photograph an actress might have in her portfolio.

Or an escort.

Obviously thinking the same thing, Gabe copied the number onto a small pad of paper he slipped out of his pocket and asked, "So what kind of a manager do you think Woo is?"

"A bad one, according to Mae's mother."

"Mae was a bad actress," Gabe told her. "At least according to the couple of reviews I dug up on the Net. Mrs. Chin is simply out of touch with reality concerning her daughter. What I meant was…which of Mae's careers did Woo manage?"

"Let's find out." Renata picked up the telephone and put it to her ear. "Still has a dial tone."

"You're going to call him?"

"That's the direct method." Renata dialed the number but got a startling voice mail message, which she repeated for Gabe. "Leave your name, number and measurements?"

"Hmm, now why didn't I think of using a line like that?" he asked, raising his eyebrows.

Wondering if Gabe was *trying* to be charming or if it simply came naturally, Renata laughed. "On your answering machine or in person?"

"I don't know. What do you think?"

Trying to get serious, she said, "What I think is that message doesn't tell us anything for sure."

"True. It could apply to either profession."

"I'll try again later and see if I can find out for certain."

They left the apartment the way they'd found it and locked the door behind them.

"What do you have on the escort service?" Gabe asked as they descended the stairs.

"Only that it's called Lotus Blossoms and that it works off a Web site."

The sun had set while they were in Mae Chin's

apartment, and the street was cast in a deep gloom. It was that odd time of day when everything had a surreal cast and the imagination came into play.

Such as her feeling that curious eyes were following their progress down the street.

"But you think there's a Chinatown connection?" Gabe asked.

Renata was busy checking out the street in every direction. No one suspicious that she could see.

"There's definitely an Asian link," she said, trying to relax. "Lotus Blossoms…the escorts featured on the site are of Asian descent. As to Chinatown itself, I wouldn't be surprised."

"So what could Mae Chin have gotten on Fred Woo?"

"Proof of illegal activities, I imagine. Chinatown's had a history of gambling and smuggling operations, among other things."

"You mean drugs."

"Actually, I was thinking of herbs." Probably because they were passing another herb shop, this one dark and seemingly deserted. "Things used for medicinal purposes that are illegal in this country. The Chinatown Chamber of Commerce has made it a priority to clean up its streets, but criminals never give up until they're put behind bars. They merely go farther underground."

"Or take cover under a semi-legitimate operation like an escort service," Gabe offered.

"That's one business I would like to close down. Not that S.A.F.E. would ever be involved in that kind

Chapter Six

"Do you gentlemen have a problem?" Gabe asked more calmly than he was feeling.

"You're the problem," Spike said, while Pigtail simply gave him a small bow and took the position.

Great. He could hold his own in a street fight, but he was no martial arts expert. He had the feeling this guy was—maybe both of them were.

"I suggest you move on," Renata said, flashing her badge. "Unless you want trouble."

"Trouble is my middle name," Spike said with a grin.

Gabe just bet it was. He gauged the two men, hoping to find a weakness.

"So give us your purse," Spike said to Renata, holding out his hand.

"I don't think so."

"Then I'll have to take it."

The man lunged for Renata, who whipped out of the way. Gabe grabbed his arm to swing him around and into his friend, but got a kick in the side for good measure.

"Who put you up to this?" Renata asked. "How much did he pay you? I can pay more for you to give us a name, then leave us alone."

Spike simply grinned and went after her again. Gut tightening in response, Gabe stepped between them to stop him, but the much larger Pigtail grabbed Gabe with enormous strength and threw him against a parked car, setting off the alarm.

"Gabe!" Renata called out, sounding properly horrified. He grunted in return.

Seeing that she was still dancing away from Spike, he threw himself back at Pigtail. He landed a few shots before a meaty fist caught him in the side of the head. Blinded with pain, he pummeled the guy in the gut and heard him curse in some Chinese dialect as he staggered backwards. Gabe went after him and got a few more shots in before Pigtail got in a fast, sharp kick to Gabe's side that literally took away his breath.

He went down to the pavement.

Renata went after the smaller guy, kicking him at the back of the knee so he stumbled forward.

Before Gabe could stand up, Pigtail's foot was coming at him again. He grabbed hold and twisted and the man yowled and went down hard. Satisfaction was short-lived. Thick legs snapped out and locked around Gabe's neck and nothing he could do would budge them. His air supply suddenly was cut off and everything started to waver before his eyes.

"Let go of him or I'll shoot!" he heard Renata yell.

Other people were yelling, too, both in English

and in Chinese, but Gabe couldn't make out what they were saying. The pressure didn't let up. Barely aware of a scuffle next to him, Gabe was having all he could do to simply hang on and not pass out.

He saw movement…Spike knocking into Renata just as a high-pitched *thwang* seared his ears.

Something wet flashed in his face and the thick legs jerked open, freeing him, and Pigtail wailed loudly in Chinese. Gabe shook his head. His vision cleared in time to see droplets of blood spray around him. Spike! He turned quickly even as the smaller of their attackers ran across the street and practically flew over a locked iron gate. Gabe lost no time in going after him, but by the time he straddled the iron gate and peered into the parking lot, Spike was gone. Gabe ran to back up Renata.

"Move and I'll shoot again," Renata threatened the man still writhing on the ground.

Gabe focused on Pigtail, who was holding his thigh where Renata had shot him.

"That shot was kind of close, don't you think?" Gabe asked, meaning the shot had come too close to *him* for comfort.

"Sorry," Renata said without taking her eyes off the wounded man. "I was aiming for his chest."

"You missed."

UNIFORMED OFFICERS and paramedics took care of the Chinese man whose name supposedly was Sam Wong. He didn't seem like a Sam to Renata—she hadn't heard him utter a word of English other than his name. Or maybe he was playing as if he couldn't speak English because he thought he could better protect himself.

As the medics were loading the thug into the ambulance, Renata anxiously told Gabe, "You should let the paramedics look at you."

After what he'd been through, she wanted in the worst way to put her arms around him, but she didn't dare lest she break apart. That's the last thing she would do in front of him or anyone else.

"I'm fine. Breathing and everything."

"This isn't the time to joke—"

"It's the perfect time for a little humor. Better than feeling sorry for myself."

"You're sure you're all right?"

"Maybe a couple of bruises," he admitted. "If I feel any distress later, I promise you'll be the first to know. What about you?"

She felt his concerned gaze on her and remembered the way he'd tried to protect her. Warmth spilled through her and she choked out, "I'm okay."

"Well, later, if you feel weird or anything, just yell." He lifted one eyebrow at her and said, "I've always wanted the opportunity to play doctor."

Renata almost smiled. Gabe was incorrigible. If she hadn't shot Sam Wong, or whatever his real name was, he might have killed Gabe.

A civilian, and *she'd* brought him into this.

She didn't want to think too closely on the more personal aspect of her feelings in the matter, but she found that while Gabe's teasing soothed her guilt at having gotten him into this situation, it also heightened the escalating attraction between them.

This wasn't good, she told herself.

She didn't trust Gabe. But he'd put himself into the fray for her…

As they gave their statements to the local police—basically that two men had tried to rob them and then had turned violent—Renata wondered whether someone at the CPD would tie this incident with the first. Neither man had indicated they'd been sent to kill her, and they hadn't had any weapons other than their hands and feet—though in Pigtail's case, that had been enough. Spike had ordered her to give over her purse, which indicated a robbery and which meant the CPD wouldn't be breathing down her neck about the encounter unless someone did connect the two incidents.

If that happened, Renata would have to face those ramifications to her career that she feared. No way could she avoid them.

By rights, she should call in the attack to S.A.F.E. herself. She wasn't in the mood for a dressing-down by a man who hadn't acknowledged that someone tried to kill her the other night, simply because he was angry with her for admitting the truth about his burying the report when a reporter had waylaid her. Certain she would get no backup there, she stubbornly refused to make the call. She hated that Mulvihill had put her in this position.

Renata didn't argue when Gabe insisted he take her to Club Undercover for a drink or three. She felt wound as tight as a rubber band. She needed to loosen up before she got into it with him. She was going to have to tell him to back off, that she'd changed her mind. Maybe after almost getting killed, he would have a change of heart and be happy to do so. Only somehow, she didn't think so.

"So who were they working for?" she mused as they headed for the club.

"My guess would be Fred Woo," Gabe said. "Those thugs were pretty determined to get your purse from you. Maybe he thought you found whatever it was that Mae Chin was using to blackmail him."

"But how could he even know we were at her place?"

"Maybe he had it staked out."

"That doesn't make sense," Renata said. "If he wanted to find whatever she was holding over him, he could have broken in and gotten it himself a week ago!"

"Whoa. You do need a drink."

While she figured she could down a couple of fingers of anything straight, Renata decided to act civilized and order a Cosmopolitan when Gabe delivered her to the bar.

On second thought...

"Make that a triple," Renata told Blade. The bartender was alone, taking stock of the bar before the club opened.

"I'm hoping not to have to carry you to get you home," Gabe said.

"You're the one who insisted on bringing me to the club for a drink. But all right. A double."

"Double Cosmopolitan coming right up," Blade said, retrieving a martini glass.

"And you need to drink that with food." Gabe was cutting across the club. "Don't start without me."

"Where are you going?"

"To raid the kitchen for anything edible."

Renata didn't argue with him. Though she felt more stressed than hungry, she knew drinking on an empty stomach would be a mistake. She didn't need to be sick or pass out on top of everything else.

Club Undercover wouldn't open for another half hour, and staff members were rushing around, getting everything in order. So Renata was surprised when an attractive woman with mahogany-red hair and wearing a slinky purple dress that showed off her very long legs took the stool next to her.

"Hi, we haven't met. I'm Cassandra Freed, one of Gabe's colleagues."

She held out a hand with long purple nails. Renata shook and said, "I'm Renata—"

"Agent Renata Fox. I know who you are, even though Gabe's been holding out and hasn't properly introduced us." Cassandra narrowed her thick-lashed, pale gray eyes at Renata and studied her for a few seconds before nodding. "You really do need our help."

"Gabe's been talking about me?" A fact that immediately raised Renata's hackles.

"He hasn't said anything. I saw you walk in with him, is all."

Not so easily appeased, Renata said, "You knew who I was."

"I read newspapers and watch broadcast news."

"And she knows things about people," Blade said, setting Renata's drink down before her.

"Knows things?" Renata echoed.

"It's a curse," Cassandra said with a shrug of her bared shoulders.

Renata took a long swallow and felt the alcohol soothe its way down into her stomach.

Right, her name was Cassandra, like the ancient Greek prophetess, and she knew "things."

"So what do you do around here?" Renata asked as the alcohol bounced from her stomach straight to her head.

"A little of this and a little of that—hostessing, magic tricks, trying to save lives." Cassandra gave her a wry smile. "You don't believe me, do you?"

Not knowing what to believe, Renata took another swallow of her drink and asked, "About the saving lives or the psychic thing?"

"Well, I don't know if I would call it that, exactly, but yes, the second. Not surprising, though. You're a person who sees things in black or white. No shades of gray for you. If you can't see it, you don't believe it."

Renata glanced at Blade who leaned back, arms crossed over his chest, simply listening. Apparently, he was in tune with this woman.

"You have a good patter going, Cassandra. You could make a living as a fortune-teller."

"It doesn't work that way. I can't actually tell someone how their life is going to turn out. I get impressions, not always clear as to the meaning."

"No, they wouldn't be, would they?" she asked, an edge to her voice.

Cassandra raised her eyebrows and slid off her stool. "All right, then, I'll just leave you to your drink."

"Wait." Wondering if she could possibly be for real, Renata put her hand on the other woman's arm. "Look, I've had a rough afternoon. Don't leave."

"I try to help people," Cassandra said.

"So do I. Sit, please. To tell the truth, I don't know if it's the alcohol or the conversation, but this is the best I've felt all day."

"Soon you're going to feel even better," Gabe promised, sliding a plate onto the bar and inserting himself between her and Cassandra. "Once you get some food in you."

Not knowing if he'd betrayed her confidence or not, Renata had to force herself to pay attention to the food. "Smells good."

"Best potato-crusted chicken in town. So what have you two been chatting about?"

What was his voice so tight about? Renata wondered, taking a bite of the chicken. She dug in.

Cassandra said, "Your colleague and I were simply getting to know each other."

"Colleague?" Gabe repeated.

"What? I was just saying hi."

Talking with her mouth full, Renata asked, "What am I missing here?"

"Nothing!" they both said at once.

She swallowed. "I don't need ESP to tell me that's not exactly true. So spill."

Renata didn't think Gabe would, but then he caved. "Remember I said there were a few people at the club who could help you?"

"Right. You told me Blade there used to be Special Ops."

Renata glanced at him and Blade gave her a thumbs-up. Suddenly that newfound appetite was lost. She set down her fork and stared at Gabe meaningfully.

He cleared his throat. "Well, Blade and the owner, Gideon, and Cass and I have had some experience helping people out of jams in the past."

"So you're all what?" Renata asked, looking around from one to the other. "Private investigators?"

"Not exactly. I wanted to tell you before but I didn't think you would be too receptive."

Renata listened in amazement as Gabe gave her a rundown of cases handled by Team Undercover. Helping an escaped convict find the real murderer. Protecting a woman who'd been kidnapped and threatened with death. Proving that the prime suspect in a murder case was innocent.

By the time Gabe was through, Renata was wondering what in the world she'd gotten herself into simply by agreeing to let him tag along with her.

"Don't look at me like I have two heads," Gabe pleaded.

He was wearing his charming smile, but this time Renata wasn't impressed. She was worried that she'd made a huge mistake in agreeing to anything. That handcuff idea was looking better and better. Her idea, not his.

"Why didn't you tell me all this before, Gabe?"

"I tried to, but you weren't receptive to my bringing anyone else in, so I figured it could wait."

"Until what? Until I got desperate enough to do whatever you suggested? For Pete's sake, I only agreed to let you in a couple of hours ago!" she said heatedly. "What else are you planning behind my back?"

Though Renata hated the feeling that she'd been tricked, she tried to keep her temper in check.

"Listen, if you want to check us out with someone you can trust," Cassandra said, "talk to Detective John Logan or Detective Stella Jacobek. They're both in Area 4 now."

"Jacobek?" Renata echoed.

"Right."

Renata looked from Cassandra back to Gabe. "I don't appreciate being conned."

"What are you talking about?"

"You put Stella Jacobek up to calling me."

"Stella called you?" Cassandra asked. "When?"

"Today." As if she didn't know.

"Renata, honestly, we haven't brought her in on this," Blade said. "She must have called because she was assigned your case and was following up after the attack."

"We," Renata echoed, looking from Blade to Cassandra to Gabe. She noticed *he* hadn't denied it, and was trying to cover an expression that looked an awful lot like guilt. "Meaning you brought them in on this case, even though you weren't in on the case."

"You don't understand. They knew about the case before I offered my services," Gabe said. "That's it."

Hating the fact that he'd lied to her—or that he'd not told her everything at the very least—she slid off the stool. "I'll see myself home."

"I don't think so." Gabe stood in her way, his expression serious for once. "You're not safe."

"I can take care of myself."

"And now whoever is after you knows that and won't underestimate you again."

A shiver crept up her spine. "So what do you suggest I do about it?"

"Come home with me."

Renata laughed and shook her head. "You're a trip, Gabriel Connor, but I'm off this train."

She headed for the door, but he was right behind her. When he took her arm in a deceptively light grip, she was tempted to show him what a bad idea touching her could be…but she couldn't bring herself to do it. She'd had enough violence in the last few days. She didn't exactly trust Gabe, but he had put himself on the line for her—she couldn't forget that.

That thought calmed her enough so that she got in his car without further argument.

But the fifteen-minute drive to her place was anything but soothing. Tension wired between them. Tension that increased when he found a parking spot right in front of her building and insisted on coming up with her. Though it was built to hold about a dozen people, the elevator car felt too small with him in it.

"How much do you trust me?" he asked suddenly.

"About as far as I can throw you."

"After seeing you in action this evening, I would bet that's pretty far, then."

"You'd be wrong."

He pushed it. "Am I?"

The elevator stopped on the third floor and the doors opened. Renata stepped out, feeling as if he were breathing down her neck when he followed her to her door.

"This is over, Gabe. You're off the case."

"No."

"I'm serious."

"So am I."

Why couldn't he just back off and simplify her life?

"I trust you want to help sort out the truth," she said. "I don't trust why."

"I told you—"

"Only what you want me to know. Some mysterious person you cared about was needlessly killed. I get that. But just as sure as you left out the fact that you weren't alone in this, you've left out identifying that person."

His response—"Trust yourself, Renata"—irritated her.

"What does that have to do with you?"

"You trusted your instincts when it came to the City Sniper. Despite all the opposition, you went on with your own investigation. You even accepted my help. If you thought I was a danger to you, you would've steered clear. You have good instincts. Trust *them*."

He was so close she couldn't think clearly. When he turned it on, his appeal was compelling. She *wanted* to trust him. Did that mean she was sure of her own instincts? Or merely being foolish?

Truth be told, she needed to trust someone. She was too new at this. Too uncertain of her own skills. Too afraid she would miss something.

But she wasn't afraid or uncertain of her instincts.

In the end, she said, "What choice do I have?"

"Not exactly the ringing endorsement I was hoping to hear, but I'll take it."

They stood at her door at an impasse until Gabe's stare got to her. His lids lowered over his green eyes, and his expression shifted to one that twisted her insides and made it hard to breathe.

What was wrong with her?

How could she possibly be so attracted to someone who'd been conning her?

He touched her face and she felt burnt where skin met skin. Her pulse accelerated so fast she could hear the whoosh of blood through her head and feel the thump of her heart against her breastbone.

She couldn't help herself. As if mesmerized, she reached out and touched him, as well. Her palm met his chest and she felt a heartbeat that rivaled her own.

"You saved my life tonight," he said softly. Thanks. I owe you."

"You don't owe me anything, not when you could have been killed defending me."

"On the contrary."

He stepped closer, crushing her hand between them so she could feel heartbeats in tandem.

"I got you into this!" she gasped. "A civilian."

"And interested party. And I got myself here, re-member. That person I told you about—the one killed because he was in the wrong place at the wrong time—was my kid brother Danny. He was shot to death."

Renata blinked and her eyes stung with the pooling of tears. So he did know what it was like to lose someone he loved to violence. Her dad…his brother…a connection that moved her.

"Oh, Gabe, I'm so sorry."

"I do believe you are," he murmured, tracing the corner of her eye with his thumb.

She turned her head into his hand, pressed her cheek to his palm, and it was then, when she felt soft and vulnerable and teary-eyed, that he kissed her. Not the deep, wet kiss of a lover, but the gentle brush of his lips over across hers. Another brush, this one less tentative, but as if he were giving her the chance to pull away. When she didn't, he took her more fully in his arms and his mouth covered hers, as if demanding entrance.

She gave way, opening to him, gladly receiving the thrust of his tongue. Her body responded, quickly awakening, acknowledging that she was still alive. That they both were. They'd beat a life-or-death situation and the importance of that hit her fully only now.

Gooseflesh spread along her limbs as she imagined just how they could celebrate. Her nipples tightened in anticipation.

For a moment, she thought Gabe might do more than simply touch her. For a moment, she thought he might try to seduce her right here in the hallway.

And then, just as Renata was going to reach around behind Gabe, unlock the door and push him inside where they could undress each other, Gabe let go of her and backed off.

Renata stood there, staring at him for what seemed like forever, until he backed off farther toward the elevators, one hand raised. She couldn't believe that he meant to go.

A reprieve.

For the moment.

She wouldn't bet this one kiss was all there would be between them.

HE WAITED IN the shadows across from the Fox woman's apartment building, not knowing why he was still here. Never return to the scene of the crime unless the circumstances necessitate doing so. He'd broken his own rule. That's what came of looking for the easy way out.

Of course, he thought she'd be easy. Unaware and unprepared.

Perhaps she was charmed. Whatever her edge, it was working for her...for now.

He saw the man who'd escorted her home the last two nights and who had helped create the debacle in Chinatown leave the building.

Not a lover, then.

Good. No personal interest. Probably a hired bodyguard.

The man stopped at his car and beeped it unlocked. He even opened the door. But then he stood there, as if he sensed something amiss. Warped light shone down on the man's face, illuminating features that were familiar if not readily identified.

Where had he seen them before?

It would come to him, he thought, as the man finally slid behind the wheel and swung the door shut.

After the car pulled away from the curb, he gave thought to entering the building and Renata Fox's apartment. But no doubt she had locked up as tight as a fortress. And no doubt she slept with her gun under her pillow.

He would have to catch her unawares...the bodyguard, too...

There was always tomorrow.

Chapter Seven

Renata lost sleep over the Chinatown incident and the knowledge that Gabe had told strangers her business against her wishes. And she'd lost that sleep over Gabriel Connor himself.

If he hadn't backed off last night....

Her head might tell her one thing about getting closer to him, but her body seemed to have its own mind. She tossed and turned and wondered what making love with him would have been like. Bad enough that he distracted her when they were together. Now he was disturbing her dreams.

The next morning, tired and cranky, she arrived at the office to find a young blond reporter had discovered the back way in via the loading dock.

"Agent Fox," the reporter said, getting between her and the door. "The public would like an update on your report about the City Sniper."

"No comment."

"After raising all this fuss in the media, you have no comment? Surely there's something you want to say to justify your stance."

"Please move away from the door," Renata ground out, trying at least to pretend to be polite.

"Has your job been threatened?"

Renata wanted to threaten the reporter. She was in no mood for this. Instead of arguing with her, she marched around the front way and past several other media types who were still camped in the vestibule.

"Agent Fox, wait!"

"How has your report affected your status with S.A.F.E.?" asked a man who stuck a mike in her face.

"Is the investigation ongoing?"

"No comment!"

Luckily, the security guards held the reporters at bay while Renata escaped through the metal detectors and into an elevator. To further her bad mood, Tag Garvey was sitting on the edge of her desk waiting for her.

Great. What a way to start her day.

She forced a smile. "What can I do for you, Tag?"

"Not a thing. I'm simply delivering a message."

"From?"

"Director Mulvihill. He wants to see you ASAP. You screwed up big-time, Fox." Tag slid off her desk and stepped closer to her in what she considered a threatening manner. "The only thing I regret is that I couldn't have the pleasure of blowing the whistle on you myself."

"For what?"

"You shot a man yesterday."

Renata started. She hadn't expected anyone here to know yet. "In the line of duty."

"Really?" Tag's grin widened. "Don't keep the boss waiting."

Aware that keeping Mulvihill waiting wouldn't be politic, Renata did an about-face. She hated giving Tag the upper hand and a reason to gloat. But what else was she to do?

On the way to Mulvihill's office, she tried not to panic. She'd been prepared for this. She just hadn't expected the information to get channeled the director's way so fast. She pulled out her cell phone to check for messages. Of course there was one from an unhappy sounding Mulvihill.

She slipped the cell into her pocket and entered the man's office.

The director was on the telephone and he held out a hand, indicating she should wait. The call sounded personal. His wife, she thought, tuning out. Mulvihill kept her waiting and wondering for several minutes. When he hung up the phone, he didn't seem in any hurry to get to her. Busying himself with some folders on his desk, he kept her standing there like a student who'd just earned a detention.

Biting back her irritation, she calmly said, "Sir, I was told you wanted to see me?"

Mulvihill flicked her a glance, closed the folder he'd been perusing so casually and asked, "What the hell happened last night?"

"I defended myself in an attack."

"What were you doing in Chinatown during work hours?"

He already knew the answer to that, Renata thought, saying, "Following up on the sniper case."

"The case is closed."

"I don't agree."

"You aren't in charge."

"Sir, I respectfully ask that you hear me out." Renata sucked in a big breath, then pitched him rapid-fire. "I take my work very seriously. I take my commitment to the people of this country equally seriously. You gave me a job to do and I intend to see it to its end."

Mulvihill drummed his fingers on the desktop and stared at her for a moment before asking, "Are you telling me you won't quit poking around, even though I've closed the case and ordered you to move on?"

Renata thought it provident that she not respond.

"Very well, then," Mulvihill said. "I'm going to suggest you take a couple of personal days to cool off. If you don't, you'll leave me no choice but to suspend you from active duty until this situation is sorted out."

"But, sir, there are protections—"

"Not in this case, because I wouldn't be suspending you for blowing the whistle on the operation. The suspension would reflect your refusal to take orders. It's called insubordination."

Considering the circumstances, Renata knew she wouldn't have a leg to stand on. And even if she did, recent history had shown it was nearly impossible to prove one was being punished for whistle-blowing to the court's satisfaction.

"I'll be glad to take a few personal days."

"I thought you might. And while you're off, think about what you've done," he said, as if she were a naughty child. "You have no loyalty, Fox. The people you work with are the same people who watch your back. But you have to earn their trust. You can't betray them and expect them to support you. As it is, who's going to watch your back now?"

He was correct, of course. She was alone in this, at least at S.A.F.E.

Now she knew how her dad had felt when accusations had been made about him. She didn't want to think about how the scandal had affected him. How it had all ended.

In the meantime, there was no use arguing with Director Mulvihill or with Paul Broden or with Tag Garvey, who was taking such a negative personal interest in her situation.

Thankfully, she had Gabe to watch her back.

And maybe his friends, as well, she conceded.

While she'd poked around the apartment the night before, straightening things that needed no straightening, cleaning things that were already clean, she'd thought about Gabriel Connor and Team Undercover, as he'd so jokingly referred to his colleagues.

Truth be told, she'd liked the talkative Cassandra despite the mumbo jumbo thing the woman had going on. And Blade had seemed quietly in control—his Special Ops training, no doubt. She hadn't met Gideon, so she had no opinion of him, but the others seemed to respect him. And despite her protests to the contrary, she did trust Gabe, at least in the respect that he wanted to help her.

Therefore, she should trust them all, right? And five heads were better than two. All combined, they could cover a lot of ground in a few days.

It ate at her that she had to do this. That she couldn't count on her own agency to back her. And she knew she was taking a big chance bringing in outsiders.

But what were her options? To drop the ball? To leave herself open to someone who probably would want her dead even if she stopped the investigation?

Renata wouldn't feel safe until she'd caught whoever was trying to shut her up permanently.

Maybe she would feel more confident about involving even more people if she called one of the Chicago detectives who apparently knew so much about Gabe's undercover activities.

Almost to her cubicle, she literally ran into Paul Broden.

"Whoa," he said, steadying her. "Where's the fire?"

"I'm being sent home."

"Suspension?"

"I was given the opportunity to take a couple of personal days." Not that Mulvihill meant for her to continue the investigation, of course. Noting a thin, dark-haired woman sitting near her cubicle, twisting her hands together, Renata asked, "Who's the woman?"

"Don't worry about it. I'll take care of her."

"Broden…"

Reluctantly, he said, "Her name's Marlene Bourne."

"As in victim number five's sister?"

"That would be the one."

"Why is she here?"

"She asked to see you, but I can take care of her. Go. Get while the going is good."

Renata was torn between protecting her job and wanting to get to the truth. As always with her, truth won.

"I'll talk to Ms. Bourne before I go."

Broden shrugged. "It's your career."

Renata could tell he didn't approve. But she was doing a lot her colleagues disapproved of these days. Praying that Mulvihill didn't get wind of this encounter, Renata approached Heidi Bourne's sister.

"Ms. Bourne, I'm Agent Fox. How can I help you?"

Marlene Bourne rose and straightened the pleats of her skirt. "I saw the news," she said in a hushed tone. "You don't think the Hawass man killed my sister, right?"

She should evade the question, Renata supposed. "No, I don't."

"Me, neither."

Figuring the woman was here to discuss her own suspicions, Renata asked, "Would you like to get a cup of coffee away from here?"

"Absolutely."

"Give me a minute to get my things."

Renata was quick but not quick enough. They were waiting for the elevator when Mulvihill came out of his office. Great. His forehead puckered into a frown as he stared at them. Renata guiltily looked away and breathed her relief as the elevator doors opened. She followed Marlene Bourne into the car and hit the button for the lobby.

A few minutes later, they were seated at the coffee bar across from the S.A.F.E. building, and Marlene was reminiscing about her sister.

"Heidi was a good if misguided person. She was easily influenced, and Carl Cooper wasn't what he made himself out to be to his constituents."

The only thing Renata knew about Congressman Carl Cooper was that he'd headed the committee that had funded S.A.F.E. That and the scandal involving use of government monies to entertain foreign dignitaries in a less-than-dignified fashion. Heidi Bourne had made the arrangements for the parties and in return had received designer clothing and jewelry, both paid for from U.S. coffers. To save herself from doing time, she'd made a deal to testify against her employer. Only she wouldn't be doing that now.

"Well, the legal system will take care of Congressman Cooper," Renata said, hoping that was true.

"How?" The woman worried her cup so that the coffee sloshed against its sides. "I don't believe Cooper will stand trial for murder."

"Murder?" *Heidi?* "You don't think—"

"I'm afraid I do. Cooper threatened my sister. He

told her she would never testify against him, and now she won't be able to, will she?"

"That doesn't make Cooper a murderer."

"If you really think her death was a coincidence, then you're naive. And you've disappointed me." Marlene Bourne shook her head and stood. "I'm sorry for wasting your time."

"Wait. I'm still investigating," Renata said, knowing she wasn't going to let go until she got to the truth. "Leave me your telephone number. I, or someone else, may contact you for more information."

She didn't add that "someone else" might not be from S.A.F.E.

Marlene hesitated, then gave Renata her card. "You're really continuing the investigation?"

Renata nodded. "And I don't intend to stop until I get to the truth."

"All right then." Marlene dug into her large bag and pulled out a small book, which she handed to Renata. "My sister's address book. She must have dropped it in my car the day before…"

Renata nodded. "I won't let you down."

She had to come through for Mrs. Chin, for Marlene and for anyone else who'd lost a loved one, which brought her to another decision.

Waiting only until the woman was out of sight, Renata pulled out her cell and got the number of the CPD area office and asked to speak to Detective Stella Jacobek.

Within minutes, the detective confirmed everything Gabe had told her about Team Undercover.

"I know this has gotta be weird for you," Stella said. "It was for me, the first time I got involved. I didn't even know what I was getting into. But recently, a friend of mine who was up on bogus murder charges needed some serious help. Blade and Cass and Logan and Gideon all came through for me. They've all got different areas of expertise. Logan's another Chicago detective, for example, and Blade was in Special Ops."

A reassurance that Renata needed to hear. "Doesn't this bother you, though?" she asked. "I mean you *are* a member of Chicago's finest. Doesn't this go against the grain as an officer of the law?"

"The first time didn't make me too comfortable relying on citizens. But I saw the value. There are some things in my position I can't do. And when official heat came down on Dermot, I knew I would do whatever it took to help him. Gabe and the others… they're all good people. They'll go to the mat for you."

The next call Renata made was to Gabe.

AFTER CHOWING DOWN on an early dinner, Gabe picked up Renata to continue their investigation. The club could do without him for a few hours. And he could do with some time spent with the woman who was wreaking havoc with his peace of mind. Her sitting in the car with him was distracting. He noted the flash of flesh as she adjusted her legs—as usual she was wearing a skirt—and then he had to adjust himself.

He'd kissed her the night before and since one thing often led to another, who knew where that might have landed him if he hadn't forced himself away from her. In her bed, to be specific.

What had he been thinking?

If Renata knew the real reason he'd involved himself in her problems in the first place... Not that he'd lied to her. His brother Danny *had* been killed for no reason. He simply hadn't told her the whole truth—the details of how Danny had been killed and why. If he had, she would never have agreed to his working with her.

Better to keep his mind on the prize, a challenge where Renata was concerned.

The sky was cloudy, the north side Ravenswood Manor neighborhood dark when they arrived at the Hudson residence. The stately old two-story brick house had mullioned windows and stood on a large lot that led right to the Chicago River and a private dock.

"Successful husband," Renata murmured as Gabe pulled into the drive.

"Successful and abusive and now very dead," he mused.

And, indeed, Janice Hudson didn't seem to be the grieving widow.

Muffled laughter spilled out of the house as Gabe rang the doorbell. And when she answered the door, the woman herself looked as if she'd had a makeover. Renata had told him she'd been subdued and red-eyed when she'd interviewed her the week before.

But the only thing red now was her dress and matching lipstick.

She seemed to have gotten over her grief quickly.

"Do I know you?" the widow asked, her expression perplexed as she looked from one to the other.

"Agent Renata Fox. We met a few days after your husband was murdered."

Janice Hudson's smile faltered. Rather than letting them inside, she stepped out onto the stoop and pulled the door closed behind her. Gabe figured she didn't want her guests to hear what they had to say.

"I thought that mess was all settled."

Mess? If that's how she thought of her late husband, then maybe he really was on to something.

"Not quite settled, no," Gabe said smoothly. "We're still trying to get a handle on the motive for the crime."

"I thought the shootings were random and that Hawass was a terrorist."

"That may be," Renata said. "But we're simply double-checking for any other connections."

"I don't understand. You think Hawass might have *purposely* killed my husband?"

"That's one possibility."

Janice Hudson's face pulled into an unattractive expression. "What does it matter now, anyway?" she demanded. "Gary is dead and so is the sniper! Close the case, already. I want to get on with my life!"

Appearing startled by the other woman's vehemence, Renata said, "If you'll just answer some questions—"

"I suggest you contact my lawyer."

With that, the widow took herself inside and slammed the door in their faces.

"Well, that was abrupt," Renata muttered.

Gabe sank into a thoughtful silence as they climbed back into the car and he pulled out of the driveway. Renata had told him about Marlene Bourne's claims earlier and he was drawing a conclusion they hadn't before discussed.

"You're quiet," Renata said.

"Just putting one and one together."

"And getting?"

"Two. Maybe three or four."

"You're talking about connections?"

"Maurice Washington had a silent partner who benefited from his death," Gabe said. "And Mae Chin had some information that was going to get her out of her contract, information that might have put her manager at risk. Now you tell me Carl Cooper threatened Heidi Bourne and her sister thinks the congressman had her murdered—"

"And if we take it a step farther," Renata mused, "when Gary Hudson was shot, his wife Janice conveniently lost an abusive husband."

"She didn't seem to be grieving, you noticed."

"I noticed."

"What if the connection is that in each case, the shooter was hired to kill one of the victims?"

"No one ever brought up that theory before. Hmm. The sniper a hired killer."

"A very clever killer," Gabe went on. "What if he

made it seem like his sniper activities were random shootings, while in reality, they were planned murders. And when Hawass was shot by the S.A.F.E. team, he stopped. He knew that no one would be looking for him if the murders didn't continue."

"But if he's a hit man—"

"He could be multitalented, use other weapons."

"True enough," Renata agreed, sounding like she was warming to his theory. "But he couldn't have counted on Hawass being shot. Could he? Unless…"

"Unless the shooter set up Hawass. Or possibly someone wanted *Hawass* dead—therefore he, too, was one of the marks. His sister said he left the house after taking a phone call. And you told me that the agency got an anonymous tip…"

"And Hawass was carrying the rifle used by the City Sniper," Renata told him.

"You know that for a fact?"

"The lab confirmed it," she said. "So, then, who is our hit man?"

"Now that's a whole other question. One plus one seems to be adding up to four. It would be interesting if the last victim adds up to five."

BEING THAT SHE had no information on relatives of the bookstore clerk Chuck LaRoe, Renata conceded that they might as well leave investigating him until morning. She had the whole day to fill. And the day after that.

Rather than taking her home, Gabe insisted on bringing her with him to the club. Renata figured that since she agreed to include Team Undercover in their private investigation, he wanted to strike while the iron was hot...and before she could change her mind.

At least Renata hoped that was *all* Gabe had planned. She was too susceptible to his charm and while she'd decided to trust him with her life, that didn't mean she needed to trust him with her heart.

So when he said, "Someone is following us," she wasn't psychically prepared for the shift.

She glanced over her shoulder. "How do you figure?"

"The high-riding vehicle lights that have been behind us the last couple of miles, turns and all, are a dead giveaway," Gabe told her.

Her stomach clenched as Gabe turned again, onto a dark side street, and the other vehicle turned with them. Though she stared straight back through the rear window, she couldn't make out anything more than a dark silhouette of a truck with blindingly bright halogens.

"What's he doing using fog lights in the city?"

"For one, you can't see who's behind the wheel," Gabe pointed out. "Clever."

"When did the truck start following us?"

"I don't actually know. I've been a little distracted tonight."

Wondering about the nature of that distraction, Renata said, "So it could be a coincidence."

"Could be."

But then the truck sped up, the higher bumper of

the bigger vehicle crashed into Gabe's trunk and jerked her against her seat belt. Renata had to admit that, once again, this was no coincidence.

Chapter Eight

"Damn!" Renata threw out her hands to the dash to steady herself.

Gabe's curse was stronger and directed at the other driver. The car picked up speed but they didn't leave the other vehicle in their dust.

"Can you see the license plate?" she asked, craning around to no avail.

"No."

"I can't see anything, either. I don't think there is a plate." Another sudden turn jerked Renata toward the door. "What's the plan?"

"Beat him at his own game."

They sped down an alley to a T intersection. Renata's insides were twisted into a knot as she turned in her seat to see what the other driver would do. Behind them, the truck made a false start into the alley. The driver turned too wide, then had to back up.

When Gabe took another hard right and Renata saw where he was headed, her eyes widened—a dead end! A massive industrial building blocked the far end of the alley.

But just as quickly, he did a dizzying U-turn in an empty parking area behind it. He must have known about this, she thought. Then he reached for the dash and cut the car lights. He'd barely hit the brakes when Renata spotted the truck's brights as it approached the T.

This time it made the turn, no problem. The driver didn't stop the truck until the last second and nearly slammed into the building creating the dead end.

"Now let's see who this guy is," Gabe said, turning on the lights and nosing the car out into the truck's path, effectively blocking it from going anywhere.

Heart pounding, Renata pulled the gun from her shoulder bag, the third time in as many days. Even so, she was no more comfortable thinking about using the weapon than before. She hadn't known how much she disliked guns until she'd been faced with using hers. Shooting it at an inanimate target on a practice range was like a game, while thinking about using it on a person was grim reality.

"There's a rear license plate. I can see it's a Michigan plate," she said, "but it's covered with dirt. Can't read letters or numbers."

She undid the seat belt and was about to get out when the truck's transmission shifted and the backup lights glowed red. Gabe swore and threw the car into Reverse in the nick of time. The near-collision as the truck rocketed by them shook Renata, but she firmly grasped the gun handle and told herself she was ready for a face-off.

The chance never came. She steadied herself against the car and used both hands on the gun, but the truck kept going. And Gabe apparently chose the safe route and, rather than take chase, didn't follow.

"I probably should have tried to shoot out the tires or something," Renata said, lowering her weapon.

"With your skills, you probably would have chewed up a nearby telephone pole."

Knowing he was referring to the close call with Sam Wong, she said, "That's not fair. Wong's buddy bumped me at the last minute."

Otherwise, at that range, even *she* couldn't have missed her target.

The breath she didn't know she'd been holding whooshed out of her and Renata realized Gabe was probably trying to lighten things up—his way of dealing with a tense situation. She, on the other hand, wanted to kick something. *Hard!*

"So do we call this in?" Gabe asked.

"At least I'll let Stella Jacobek know what's happening in case something goes wrong," she said.

"Sure. Not a lot you can tell her, though. We know it was a black truck with Michigan plates. Period."

They were no closer to identifying the offender than she had been when attacked the other night. Her frustration mounted exponentially every time she was faced with a new roadblock. At least anger drove away any jitters. Rather than wanting to break down, she was ready for a fight.

"Maybe you could call one of your detective friends in the department and keep him or her informed, just in case we need someone to back us up about this later."

"Good thinking."

She whipped out her cell phone and offered it to him. "Oops. Not your thing, is it?"

He took it from her anyway.

"Want me to show you how to make a call on this baby?"

"I said I didn't own a cell phone, not that I didn't know how to use one."

Gabe's pseudoinjured tone sliced through the dark and warmed her insides. Getting even with him for that obsessive-compulsive crack was probably the only satisfaction she was going to get tonight, so she might as well enjoy it.

RENATA'S FIRST THOUGHT when she saw Gideon ensconced in his Club Undercover office was that the deep blue walls were the same shade as the incredible eyes framed by glossy magazine-handsome features and longish blue-black hair slicked back from his face.

"So this is everyone?" she asked, looking around to see Cassandra and Blade already present. "Team Undercover?"

"Those who work at the club," Gideon said.

Making her wonder if the owner considered the two detectives part of the team since they'd been major participants in other cases. Which made her wonder about her own standing—what would they expect of her?

"Renata, at last we meet," Gideon said. "Have a seat."

She nodded. "Gideon." Then took one of the two vacant chairs before the black and chrome desk, while Gabe took the other.

Gideon began, "Gabe brought me up to date—"

"I know. On *my* cell phone." She gave Gabe a sideways glance.

"They come in handy sometimes," she said, then turned back to the club owner.

A black eyebrow arched over one of those sapphire eyes but Gideon didn't comment.

Gabe picked up the ball. "I figure we must be getting close to something important."

"How do you figure?" Renata asked.

"Because now we're both on the killer's hit list. First Chinatown, now this."

"But Fred Woo—"

Gabe cut Renata off, saying, "Probably had nothing to do with the attack unless he's the mastermind behind everything. More likely, someone followed you and realized you weren't working alone."

Though she'd hoped there was no connection between the first two attacks, he could be correct. "I'm sorry. I never should have involved you."

"Stop apologizing, and again, I involved myself."

"But I didn't have to agree to take your help."

"I can be very determined when I make up my mind about something."

But why this? she wondered. Why was *this* situation so important to him? Innocent bystanders were killed every day. And she didn't think he went around willy-nilly trying to right all wrongs.

So why this time? Why Muti Hawass? *Why her?*

Clearing his throat, Gideon said, "So we have someone who drives a black truck with Michigan license plates. Does that mean anything to you?"

Renata shrugged. "Afraid not."

Gabe shared his hit man theory.

"Hmm, a Michigan hit man comes to Chicago to kill five unrelated people," Blade said. "Odd theory."

"Odd," Renata echoed, unsure of where to go with this, "but not impossible. The border is only an hour and a half away. I guess we should look deeper to see if the people we've identified as wanting the victims dead have a Michigan connection." It didn't sound likely, though she didn't want to discount Gabe's theory altogether.

"How would this guy even have known you were on his trail?" Blade asked.

She shook her head. Nothing was making sense to her in this case.

Including Gabe's saying, "You know, Renata, it may be time for you to disappear."

"What? Run away and hide with my tail between my legs? I don't think so."

"Hide in plain sight," Cassandra said. "We can give you a new identity. I can work magic in the way of a makeover."

"Makeover?" She couldn't imagine looking other than she always did.

"I wonder what you would look like as a blonde," Gabe suddenly said.

"Ridiculous."

"Redhead is more like it," Cassandra said. "Not red like mine. More subtle. A red-brown. And shorter."

"I don't think so."

"Turquoise contact lenses," Gabe added, his lips quirking. "Or maybe violet."

"What fantasy girl are you describing?" Renata asked him.

"One with a sense of humor."

So he was poking at her again. Renata narrowed her gaze at Gabe. He simply grinned in return.

"Just for the record," she said, "I am not doing a disappearing act. No hair dye. No contact lenses. No out-of-character clothing. I have some dignity."

"They say there's no dignity in death," Blade muttered.

Starting to regret agreeing to work with these people, Renata was about to say so, when Gabe put his hand on her arm. "However Renata wants to play it is fine by me. It's her case, her call."

"You call the shots," Gideon agreed.

But Renata wasn't quite believing it. Part of her suspected they would give her lip service while quietly going about their business in the way they thought best. At least they would if they were anything like Gabe. Still, she needed help from someone.

If she could do this through official channels, she

would have a task force at her disposal. That's how she would think of Team Undercover.

"All right. Then tomorrow, why don't you all follow the Michigan connection, while Gabe and I see where Chuck LaRoe leads us."

Gideon nodded and Cassandra said, "Fine with me."

"How about I follow up on the sharpshooter connection, instead?" Blade suggested. "Not that many people have the talent to do what this guy did, and I know a number of them."

"Good."

Talent—sending a bullet into someone's head. Renata shivered.

And wondered if she really had the stuff it took for this job, after all.

WHEN GABE pulled up before a multi-unit building on a side street she guessed to be about a mile from Club Undercover, Renata said, "I thought you were taking me home."

"I am. Just not to *your* home."

He peered out into the dark through every window as if making sure they didn't have visitors waiting.

But how could they know where to wait? Renata wondered. She might have been followed earlier, thereby implicating him by association, but that didn't mean the shooter or any compatriots were aware of Gabe's identity or of the Club Undercover connection.

Gabe left the car and was around it fast enough to help her out. A little shakier than she figured she ought to be, Renata found it comforting that he *wasn't*. Or at least that he didn't appear to be. Her own anger—and therefore adrenaline—had worn off long ago, and she simply felt too exhausted to deal with anything else tonight.

"So, this is your place," she asked as they entered the courtyard together. The grounds were landscaped with small trees—leafless at this time of year—and beds of fall plants and flowers that were nearly spent.

"Home sweet home. You can't go back to your apartment tonight."

Renata knew he was right. Three times was the charm. She didn't want to be a sitting duck for whoever was trying to shut her up. And she wouldn't go to her mother's home and involve her, either. So it was either a hotel or Gabe's place. The hotel wouldn't have a Gabe at her disposal, though. And somehow, even though he was the citizen and she the agent with the weapon, she felt safer with him around.

Why was that? she wondered. How had he gotten so competent at this cops-and-criminals stuff?

Not wanting to know anything that would put her off, she was reluctant to ask him.

When they got inside Gabe's second-floor apartment, Renata looked around the big, high-ceilinged room with a nice-sized kitchenette. The place was neat. Then again, there wasn't much furniture to clutter—a sofa and matching ottoman, a coffee table, one end table and two stools tucked under the counter, a small table for his computer. That was it.

No personal touches that she could see...almost

as if these were temporary digs. Or perhaps he'd moved in recently and hadn't had the time to put his stamp on the place.

"The bathroom's over here," Gabe said, indicating one of two doors along the wall. He opened the other door and pulled out a robe. "You can use this. Fresh from the laundry," he promised, draping the robe on the back of the sofa.

At which time it hit her that all interior doors were accounted for. No bedroom. This was a studio apartment. One room!

Where in the world would she sleep?

Zeroing in on what had to be a sofa *bed*, her mouth went dry. And her imagination went off-kilter. For an instant, she could see herself in bed with Gabe, the two of them struggling for top position…

Gabe broke the spell by saying, "I need a drink. What's your pleasure?"

"A glass of wine would be good." Thinking he wasn't a wine kind of guy, she said, "Or a soda would be fine."

"Wine it is."

Renata glanced out the window and found herself scouring the street for movement. Anything out of place. Her pulse threaded unevenly. How long would she have to put her life on hold? It would simply be easier, more convenient, to give up. Too bad she wasn't built that way. Her dad hadn't been either…and look where it had gotten him.

"Trust me," Gabe said, handing her a glass of ruby-red wine. "I'll make sure you stay safe."

"I'll sleep on it."

She gave the sofa bed a skewed look, then realized Gabe had noticed. His eyebrows shot up and his green eyes sparkled and his lips curved into a grin. She braced herself but he didn't say a word about the sleeping arrangements.

Still, what went unsaid made her jittery.

"Sit," he said.

If only she could, Renata thought, sitting at one end of the couch. She made sure her skirt was pulled as close to her knees as possible.

"I'm going to call Gideon and let him know we're clear."

"Fine. Whatever."

Since Gabe was on the phone, Renata pulled out her cell phone and checked for messages. Two more calls from her mom, who was getting increasingly concerned. And a text message from her sister Lucille.

where r u
m nuts

Just what she was afraid of—Mom was sitting by the telephone worrying about her.

Renata sent Lucille a text message in return.

tell m undercover
kisses

"Kisses?" came a voice too near to her ear for comfort.

Renata started. Gabe had finished his conversation and was staring at her cell over her shoulder. "Eavesdropping?"

"If that's what you want to call it."

Not about to tell Gabe that she was sending her love to her mom and sister, she shut down her phone. Let him think she was involved with someone she cared about. Then he wouldn't be making moves on her.

"So you can't go for a few minutes without something to do, huh?"

"I like to fill my time productively."

Gabe kept whatever he was thinking to himself as he sat at the other end of the couch. Nervous, Renata dropped the cell phone into her purse and saw Heidi Bourne's address book—she'd forgotten all about it until now. She pulled it out and started skimming through the pages.

"Heidi Bourne's sister gave me her address book this afternoon."

"What do you expect to find in it?"

"I don't know. Probably nothing."

"Then why are you filling time going through it?"

"I don't leave anything to chance."

"A real multitasker," he muttered.

Okay, so maybe she was. Besides that, she needed a distraction, something to occupy her thoughts before they went astray. She continued going through the pages of the address book, but nothing jumped out at her. She sneaked a glance at Gabe, who was watching her and sipping his wine. The wine. She hadn't touched it. Pausing halfway through the address book—she'd gotten to the *M*'s—she picked up her glass and took a sip.

"You have good taste in *wine*."

"Other things, too."

The way he was looking at her made Renata think the comment was meant to be personal. Warmth filled her cheeks and she wondered if he *was* going to make a pass at her. They were in an intimate situation, and she couldn't help but think about how things might turn out.

So when he asked, "Are you sorry you bucked the system yet?" the abrupt question took her by surprise.

"I might not like the results...people I work with not speaking to me or worse, yelling at me...someone trying to kill me...but no, I don't regret acting on my instincts." She took a longer swallow of wine and went back to skimming the address book. *N...O...P...*" This is more than my job. It's something I had to do. I couldn't ignore what I thought was right."

"Family trait?"

"Family trait," she echoed, checking the last pages of the address book.

When she got to *W*, she stopped. "FW."

"FW what?"

"Just the initials. And a phone number you might recognize."

She showed him the book.

"Fred Woo's number." He looked up at her. "We have a connection."

"One that makes sense," Renata said. "Congressman Carl Cooper was nailed for giving inappropriate parties on government funds."

"Which included escort services?"

"Which included escort services," Renata agreed. "Mae Chin and Heidi Bourne linked."

Gabe raised his glass of wine. "A toast, then."

Renata raised her glass and clinked it to his. "To the truth."

Taking a long sip of wine, Renata felt as if she were soaring. She'd been right to file that report. But how could the S.A.F.E. team have missed this? she wondered. Something she would have to look into.

"Success looks good on you," Gabe said. "Your dad would be proud. So tell me about him."

Renata didn't usually talk about her dad. Her mom got teary-eyed every time Renata brought him up, and her sister always changed the subject. Her friends had swept what had happened under the carpet…and their friendship pretty much along with it. Well, most of them, anyway. Her best friend Megan had remained loyal, but she'd moved away when her new husband had been promoted, his new job meaning an immediate transfer to California.

And Renata certainly couldn't talk to anyone at work about what had happened.

Maybe she could talk to Gabe.

"Dad was a wonderful man," she told him. "An outstanding cop. He was investigating a murder. Dad was certain this guy had done it, but the guy had got-

ten away with criminal activities before. Dad was
angry and told everyone it was time the man paid.
But the evidence just didn't support an arrest."

"Uh-oh."

"Yeah, uh-oh. Evidence tampering seriously
crosses the line. Only Dad wasn't the one who
crossed it. But he'd been so outspoken, fingers
pointed at him. He was the one who took the heat.
Him and us. The media got hold of the story and
hounded us. He was never able to prove his inno-
cence, because before formal charges could be
brought against him, he was killed on the job. I think
he purposely put himself in a dangerous situation
where he…"

She couldn't talk about it, after all, not without
wanting to cry. Not even after all these years. Her
eyes misted over and she took another sip of wine.

Gabe reached out and took her free hand. "Renata,
I'm sorry."

The warmth of his fingers intertwined with hers.
The simple gesture touched her as it had when he'd
offered condolences to Mrs. Chin. Gabriel Connor
might be an irritating man when he chose, but he
could also be kind.

"Wine makes me sloppy," she murmured.

"It brings out your humanity. You loved your dad
and I'm sure he loved you. You have great memories
of him. That's a lot more than some people can say."

Some people? Him?

Her turn to say, "Sorry."

For a moment, she thought he was going to deny

it. Then he shrugged his shoulders like his not having a good relationship with his own father didn't mean anything to him. Though she knew it must.

"Is there any hope things can change?" she asked.

"No—there never was. My father has been dead to me since I was a teenager. And my worst nightmare is that I become like him, bad genes and all."

A shiver shot through her at his cold, flat tone, and she wondered what had gone so horribly wrong in that relationship. Not that she was about to ask. He would tell her if he wanted her to know.

Instead, she reached out to Gabe as he had to her. Pulse picking up a beat, she touched his free hand, laced her fingers through his and squeezed. His gaze caught hers and she couldn't look away. Her breath caught in her throat just before he kissed her.

One touch of his mouth was all it took to make her pulse hum sweetly. He didn't start slowly as he had the last time but kissed her deeply with an intensity of emotion that threatened to overwhelm her. Maybe it was the connection they'd just made talking.

Maybe it was the danger they'd shared earlier. Whatever the reason, Renata knew she wanted nothing more than to spend the night in Gabe's arms.

Feeling a rising excitement taking over, she splayed her hand against his chest, felt his rapid heartbeat against her palm. Her heart was beating in sync.

And as quickly as Renata was caught up, she was released. Gabe ended the kiss and broke away, sliding back on the couch so they were no longer touching. They were both breathing heavily, gazes locked, and she would bet he was as aroused as she. So why the heck had he stopped?

His "Do you want to shower first or should I?" brought her desires down a notch.

Tempted to say *together*, she stopped herself. "*I* will."

Dazed, she pulled herself together and pushed herself up to her feet. Quickly, she grabbed the robe from the back of the couch and scurried into the bathroom.

Embarrassment…confusion…desire all warred within her.

Part of her needed the comfort of a man—this man—making love to her and sheltering her body with his through the night. Part of her thought that was the worst idea in the world. They needed to be on guard, of course. No doubt that's what Gabe was thinking. Or perhaps he assumed that after they both showered…

No, they'd been caught up in the moment—that was all. They didn't have that kind of relationship. She didn't know what to call what they did have.

She stepped into the shower and let steaming water beat down on her.

Unsure of Gabe's intentions for the night, Renata wondered what she was supposed to do when she got out of the shower.

Her practical side took over. Her needs came second to the investigation.

That's where she needed to concentrate her energies.

A little voice told her she was making excuses, that she'd done this before to keep herself emotionally distanced from men she dated and, yes, slept with.

But she didn't really want to be emotionally distant with Gabe. She wanted to share everything, the way they had if only for a moment. And that thought scared her.

Torn about what to do, what to say, she stepped out of the shower and dried off. Her skin felt alive. She felt alive. She felt…she didn't want to analyze whatever it was too closely.

That's how she always ruined things for herself—by over-analyzing.

Renata pulled on the robe and brushed out her hair so the dark strands fell like a silken waterfall against the white terry robe.

But when she opened the door, she felt her anticipation drain. Gabe had turned down the lights, and it took her eyes a moment to adjust and find him in the darkened room.

The sofa bed was wide open and inviting, but Gabe wasn't in it.

He'd made himself a bed on the floor from the discarded couch cushions.

Furthermore, he was sound asleep…

Chapter Nine

Gabe hadn't really been sleeping when Renata had come out of the shower, but he'd figured pretending to be asleep would be the smartest thing. He'd wanted in the worst way to make love to her and he was certain she'd been ready, too. But he couldn't do that to her. He'd deceived her from the first, and she didn't deserve another betrayal.

So he'd pretended. And he'd lain awake listening to her as she'd settled down trying to sleep.

He figured they'd both been awake half the night.

Now it was morning and they'd overslept. If he wasn't mistaken, Agent Renata Fox was a tad cranky this morning. He shoved a fresh cup of coffee at her, careful that their fingers didn't so much as brush together.

"Drink. It'll make a new woman of you."

"I don't need to be new. I thought I made that clear yesterday. I like myself exactly the way I am."

"Exactly?"

To her credit, she didn't take the bait. She

practically drowned herself in that single cup of coffee.

"What would you like for breakfast?" he asked.

"Never eat it."

"Ah," he said knowingly.

"I'm going to give you a pass on that one," she mumbled, shoving the cup over the counter toward him. "More coffee. Please."

He refilled her cup and raided the refrigerator for some deli turkey. Without ceremony, he slapped it in a slice of bread, which he bent in half.

"You're really going to eat that?"

"I need protein in the morning. And carbohydrates. I figured since you weren't interested in a properly prepared meal, I would go with fast."

She stuck her face back in the cup of coffee.

And Gabe couldn't help smiling as he munched on his impromptu breakfast sandwich.

Even in a sour mood, Renata was something to look at. She'd already dressed, had brushed her hair back from her face and had applied makeup. She hadn't shown herself until she looked perfect.

Hmm. Maybe he'd been on track with that obsessive-compulsive comment.

Finishing his sandwich, Gabe figured they might as well get to work. "So Chuck LaRoe had no relatives?" he asked.

"None that we could find. Not here. Not anywhere."

"A mystery man."

"So they say. People he worked with at the bookstore. Neighbors."

"Everyone in his family died or disappeared?"

"Or never existed," Renata said. "LaRoe didn't have a past we could find. It was as if he was born full-grown."

"Huh? And no one at S.A.F.E. thought that was curious?" Gabe asked.

"I wouldn't know. By the time *I* got curious, it was too late. No one wanted to talk to me."

"Let's see what we can find out."

"What do you have in mind?"

"No relatives or friends and he's been dead a little over a week. Chances are his apartment is still intact. We need to get inside."

"I don't have access to keys."

"Who needs a key," Gabe said. "All you have to do is call the building manager and tell him who you are."

But when they called the manager's office, they got a message telling them he would be out of town until Monday.

"Now what?" Renata muttered.

"Let's get going." He knew she wasn't going to like what he had in mind. "We'll find a way in."

WHEN GABE HAD blithely said they would find a way to get into Chuck LaRoe's apartment, Renata had assumed he meant they'd find a neighbor who had a key. She hadn't a clue that he'd meant to break in. But that's exactly what they were about to do. Rather, what he was trying to manage.

"If we're caught, this could mean my career," she whispered, her mouth dry.

She was standing guard in the seedy hallway of a large apartment building filled with bad smells and occasionally with worse people. Gabe was using a set of narrow tools on the lock. Not wanting to know where he got them or the expertise to use them, she didn't ask.

Gabe said, "If we don't figure out the motive and therefore identity of the sniper, you won't have to worry about a career, because you'll be dead."

"Thanks for the reminder."

The reason she was going out of bounds here. A murderer was after her. She needed to protect herself the best way she could. Still, breaking and entering wouldn't have been her first choice and didn't sit well with her.

Hearing more than one set of heavy footsteps on the stairs above coming down toward them, Renata felt the knots in her stomach tighten. Great. No doubt whoever it was would want to know what they were doing.

"Hurry up!" she urged Gabe.

She eyed the stairs anxiously, and just as the first set of legs came into view, she heard a click and him saying, "Got it. We're in."

And a second later they were. Closing the door as the patter of feet reached their landing, Renata locked it, then closed her eyes and leaned her back against the door to regain her equilibrium.

"What the hell happened here?" Gabe asked.

Renata blinked and looked around.

The place was a mess. The S.A.F.E. team had

been inside the week before, but she doubted they were responsible for the overturned chairs, the discarded dresser drawers, contents strewn across the middle of the floor or the stuffing pulled out of the couch cushions.

Renata sighed. "Looks like—if there was anything to find—we got here too late."

"If the person responsible for this mess knew exactly what he was looking for."

"You want to sort through the remains?"

"You have something better to do?" Gabe asked, after which he plunked himself down on the floor and started sifting through a pile of papers.

Rather than arguing, Renata sat down in the middle of the mess with him. Sorting through a dead man's underwear. And his socks.

Just the career move she'd dreamed of.

"Anything interesting?" Gabe asked, his tone amused.

"You're enjoying this, aren't you?"

"It's not the most challenging thing I've ever done."

"I mean me," Renata said, trying not to sound put out. "You're enjoying my reactions."

"Hey, I know you're tough. I saw you deck that Chinatown creep. This is the other side of the job."

Remembering the attack—all three attacks—she said, "I hate violence."

"Good career choice, then."

"Somehow I didn't think I would get that up-close-and-personal with the criminal element."

"What did you think you would be doing?"

"Analyzing. Interpreting. Following a paper trail," she said, throwing a pair of briefs back into a drawer.

"I see that you're doing the wrong job there." He held out a fistful of receipts. "Want to trade?"

"Too late," she said. "I'm done with the fun stuff. Now you can keep your smirks to yourself."

Renata slid closer to Gabe and starting sorting through bits of papers herself. They worked in silence for several minutes, and it actually felt good. Rather than bickering, they were working as a team.

And then, taking a good look at one of the receipts, she said, "Hold on."

"What is it?"

"A fuel slip—the receipt you get when you use a credit card to buy gas."

"Significance?"

"He bought the gas in Michigan," she said.

In her mind's eye, she could see the truck with Michigan license plates.

"Recently?"

She searched for the date and shook her head. "Last spring."

"You said there wasn't much information on LaRoe, like he sprang up out of nowhere," Gabe mused. "When would that have been?"

"Last spring."

They stared at each other.

"Look at this stuff more closely," Renata said, excitement curling through her. "Maybe we'll find more receipts from Michigan, something that can place him. If we can get a town or city, we might have a start."

For the next few minutes, they resorted and rechecked, but to no avail. The only lead to Michigan was the fuel slip and that didn't really give them any more information than that he'd been passing through the state.

And then Renata realized Gabe had stopped sorting, that he was staring intently at a piece of identification.

"You think it's something significant?" she asked, realizing how tense he'd become.

Now she was tensing, her stomach knotting, gooseflesh spreading along her body with dizzying rapidity.

And Gabe practically jumped to his feet and shoved the ID into his pocket. "It's significant," he agreed. "Let's get out of here."

"Now?"

"Now."

He gave her a hand up and Renata easily rose to her feet, stopping mere inches from him. The close contact made her breath catch in her throat. Gabe seemed unaffected, as if his mind were elsewhere.

Or as if he were putting a wall between them.

Frowning, Renata took a step back and slid the Michigan fuel slip into her shoulder bag.

Gabe was already at the door, opening it a crack and carefully peering out, as if to make certain they wouldn't be seen. Then he waved to her and opened the door. Renata flew right through and kept on for the stairs, glancing back to see him close the door and check that it was locked. As if that had stopped *him* from getting inside!

Part of her wanted to ask him about his lock-picking expertise. Part didn't want to know. And part of her simply wanted to know where they were going. She waited until they got to his car to ask.

"We're going to see a man about some fake IDs," he said as he started the engine.

"What man?" Renata demanded. "And how in the world do you know him?"

"His name is Ned Coulter and he has a shop not too far from here."

They happened to be in Edgewater, a community valued for the elevated rapid transit that ran a few blocks west of Lake Michigan. Well-heeled citizens lived east of the El in the high-rises lining Sheridan Road along the lake. Tenants of the apartment houses along the El were in a lower tax bracket. As were the people who frequented that section of Broadway, the main thoroughfare with restaurants and grocery stores and smaller shops.

They parked near Broadway Electronics, whose storefront windows boasted the best priced electronics in town.

Her mind whirling with the possible reasons Gabe might know a forger, Renata was understandably edgy. "This is where we're going to find Ned Coulter?"

"Hopefully."

"So you know him."

"We've met."

Met or done business?

Considering Gabe's reluctance to spell it out, Renata figured it had to be the latter. Feeling as if she were in a drama about to unfold, she entered the store.

The young clerk behind the counter wore headsets attached to a boombox. His hair was spiked, his jeans were ripped, his eyes were closed and his head was bobbing to whatever music he was listening to.

"Hello!" Gabe shouted.

The clerk's eyes remained closed and his head continued to bob.

Gabe whistled. Loudly.

No effect.

Finally, Gabe hitched himself over the counter and turned off the boombox.

The clerk's eyes snapped open. "Hey, whaddya think you're doing?"

"You work here?"

"Oh, yeah, right." The clerk ripped off the headsets. "What can I show you?"

"You can tell your boss he has company."

"You gotta name?"

"Yep, I sure do," Gabe said without volunteering it.

The clerk gave him a look and disappeared into the back.

"So what name does this Coulter know you by?" Renata asked.

Like the clerk had done earlier, Gabe closed his eyes and bobbed his head at her in answer.

Making her wish she could find *his* Off button. Or maybe it should be his *Play* button to make him talk. Before she could try again, the clerk appeared in the doorway and waved them back. Renata poked Gabe—a good feeling—and then took the lead around the counter to the back room.

Ned Coulter was probably in his fifties, Renata thought. He was a small, neat-looking man with a mustache, goatee and reading glasses. And, bizarrely, she thought, he was wearing a suit, even in the back room of his shop.

"Gabriel, what brings you here?" Coulter asked, all the while eyeing her. "It is still Gabriel, is it not?"

"Nothing's changed. This is Agent Renata Fox. If you're into the news, you may recognize the name."

Coulter tilted his head down so that he was looking over the reading glasses. "I recognize the face." Then he gave Gabe a long, significant look.

"We need your help," Gabe said, then added, "Renata's all right, I promise you. When we leave here, she'll forget about you. She won't involve you in anything."

Renata clenched her jaw to keep from speaking for herself. Though she had to admit, given the chance, she might have offered him the same agreement, if it was the only way to get information they could use.

"Come."

Coulter took them through another doorway into a smaller room. His desk was spread with what looked like IDs of various sorts. The skin along Renata's spine crawled. She didn't want to know about something illegal going on that she couldn't do anything about.

She didn't want to know Gabe wasn't Gabe, either, but there it was.

"What can I do for you?" Coulter asked.

Gabe said, "Chuck LaRoe."

"Never heard of him."

"Sure you did, Ned." Gabe produced the ID he'd taken from the pile on LaRoe's floor and handed it to the man. "We found this in his apartment."

Coulter shrugged. "He could have gotten this from anywhere. Ask him."

"I recognize your handiwork. And it would be a little difficult consulting with LaRoe, or whatever his name is, considering he's dead."

"I thought you paid attention to the news," Renata added, trying to hang on to her irritation. "LaRoe was one of the victims of the City Sniper." Which he had to already know considering he'd known who she was.

"What does that have to do with me?"

"You know I reopened the case," Renata said, taking over. "We've been giving the victims a closer look. Their connections, especially. We found a Michigan connection yesterday…" She purposely kept it vague. "LaRoe makes the second one. But we need to be able to put everything together and the name Chuck LaRoe doesn't do it for us."

Gabe added, "But his real name might."

"Real? How do you know if anything is real?"

Coulter looked from one to the other, then focused on her. "You're not wearing a wire, are you?"

Renata lifted her arms. "Go ahead and search me."

Gabe shoved one of her arms down and hung on to it. "She's not wired. This is between us."

The two men stared at each other long enough to make Renata even more uncomfortable. Renata lowered the other arm and released the one in Gabe's grasp, wondering how he knew they could trust Ned Coulter.

"All right," Coulter finally said. "Give me a minute." He went to his computer and typed a series of commands. Seconds later, he grunted. "His name was Russell Ackerman. And that's all I've got."

It probably was, because Gabe couldn't get anything more from the man, so a few minutes later, they gave him their thanks and left.

"Russell Ackerman. I know that name," Renata mused as she slipped into the passenger seat. "I just can't place it."

"I guess that's our next step."

This time Renata insisted they go to her place so she could get a change of clothes and her laptop. If Gabe had any objections, he kept them to himself and drove.

Leaving Renata to speculate about and brood over his association with Ned Coulter, and to wonder about his story.

Who was Gabriel Connor really...and why had he been lying to her?

GABE COULDN'T BELIEVE Renata didn't rag on him about Coulter's "It is still Gabriel, is it not?" comment. She didn't say anything, but it sat there between them like a bomb waiting to explode all the way to her place. For once he couldn't think of a way to shake the tension.

How much would he tell her?

By the time they approached her building, it was nearly noon. People were coming and going, so they lucked out and found a parking spot on the next block. Gabe kept his eyes peeled for trouble all the way to her entrance. But if anyone was staking out her place in the middle of the day, it wasn't apparent to him.

The ride up to the third floor in the elevator was as stifling as it had been the last time. Only the source of the tension was different.

No attraction here, not from her. Only suspicion. It came from Renata in waves.

How long would it take her curiosity to explode?

Once inside her apartment, he said, "Why don't you introduce me to your laptop and I'll start a search on Russell Ackerman while you change?"

Renata gave him a long look but didn't argue. "Laptop's over there."

She indicated the desk by the front windows before disappearing through an open door, which undoubtedly led to her bedroom. Before he could see inside, she slammed the door shut. Gabe took a big breath. It was like waiting for the ax to fall. He knew it was going to; he simply didn't know when.

A glance around the large room that included

living, dining and kitchen areas assured him that Renata was as organized in her home as she was about everything else. Not a thing out of place. The walls were cream, the upholstered furniture taupe; the decorative paintings and hangings in soft colors were equally soothing. Each item on the low tables near the couch and chairs was precisely placed.

As was the laptop on her extraordinarily neat desk.

Being this neat was unnatural, he thought, making himself comfortable in her chair.

He brought up a browser and search engine and typed in *Russell Ackerman* and *Michigan*. The search engine responded with dozens of links.

He'd just clicked on one when Renata came up behind him, asking, "How is it going?"

Gabe turned to see her dressed casually in jeans—tight jeans, he noted with appreciation—and a pullover in a flattering dark red. She'd brushed her hair back in a ponytail. For a moment, he simply stared. This was a whole new woman, a more relaxed version of Agent Renata Fox, a woman he'd like to get to know better. And then he realized he hadn't answered her question.

"I was just getting started, but Russell Ackerman seems to be popular on the net."

He turned back to the laptop, his gaze connecting with the LCD screen and the headline: Embry Lake Massacre Evokes Ruby Ridge Memories.

For once in his life, Gabe was shocked into silence.

"EMBRY LAKE?" Renata said, unable to keep the shock out of her voice. "No wonder I thought the name Ackerman sounded familiar. I must have read it and heard it dozens of times."

Trying to absorb this unexpected connection, she watched Gabe punch in a Find command for *Ackerman*. A second later he had it.

His voice was cold as he said, "Russell Ackerman is listed as one of the nine dead."

"*Dead?* Wait a minute. Ackerman…Leigh Anne Ackerman…his 'widow' has made a lot of noise over the deaths. What does the article say about him?"

She felt the need to sit and did so in a nearby chair. Gabe swivelled to face her.

"He wasn't shot like the others. He was one of the two who died—supposedly died, that is—in that building that burned," he said, his voice tight. "Identification of a burned corpse can be a pretty difficult proposition."

"Especially if someone saw Ackerman go into the building…or if the identities were somehow switched ahead of time," Renata said, her mind going back to Ned Coulter and his back-store business. "What if Ackerman's identification were near the body?"

"Could be," Gabe agreed. "Apparently, someone made a big mistake. At least it looks like maybe we found something we can use. Now if only we knew the significance."

"Russell Ackerman was supposed to be dead… and now he is."

"Killed while hiding in plain sight under an assumed name. The question is why."

"Maybe it had nothing to do with Embry Lake," Renata said. "Maybe Chuck LaRoe made himself a powerful enemy."

"Do you believe that?"

She didn't even have to think about it. "I don't believe in coincidences."

But she didn't know *what* to believe. Embry Lake had happened before she'd come on board at S.A.F.E., so she was not all that familiar with the case other than what she'd read and seen in the media.

The Embry Lake Brigade, a militia headed by a man named Joshua Hague, had been under scrutiny for months as being a possible link to international terrorists. S.A.F.E. had placed a man undercover there who'd sent out reports of members being held in the compound against their will.

So S.A.F.E. had used that to go in—ostensibly they were to make sure that anyone who wanted out was able to come out. Only something had gone terribly wrong and in the end, there'd been no viable link to terrorists they could find, either.

Furthermore, a few of the innocents had died along with the militia men. The final count had been seven shot, two burned to death as a result of a bullet gone astray. To make things worse, no one knew who had fired the first shot and started the massacre.

But Elliott Mulvihill, the supervising agent in charge of the operation, had been promoted to director of S.A.F.E. afterward, Renata knew.

"How familiar are you with the Embry Lake failure?" she asked Gabe.

Failure being a delicate way of putting things.

"Familiar enough," he said tersely.

"This could be a bombshell."

"What are you going to do with it?" he asked. "Bring it to Mulvihill?"

"I don't know if he would believe me. If I can't produce a source—"

"He'll bury it like he did your report."

She nodded. "My best guess."

"Then what?"

"We'll have to get proof. We'll have to go to Embry Lake ourselves."

HE CURSED as they left together. He'd been counting on the man leaving alone again, so he could get to the woman.

It seemed Agent Renata Fox was counting heavily on her bodyguard.

What she wasn't counting on was him.

The man, he'd learned, called himself Gabriel Connor. He was carrying what looked like an overnight bag and the Fox woman was carrying what he expected was her laptop. Were they going somewhere?

Not without him, they weren't.

As if he sensed they were being watched, Connor looked around, peering into shadows, as if he could see the danger he was in.

Grinning, he wanted to shout, "Look up, you big hulk." But, of course, he did no such thing.

The elevated structure continued to hide him from any observer on the street. They couldn't see him, but he could see them through the rails. Well, for the moment, anyway. Soon they would be out of sight.

Not that he was worried.

He'd found the car and had bugged it.

Wherever they went, he would be right behind them.

Chapter Ten

Anxious to get to Embry Lake, Gabe had been hard-pressed to conceal his impatience when Renata had insisted on stopping first at S.A.F.E. She'd slipped in and out of the building through the alley loading dock entrance, but had kept her own counsel about her purpose. Then she'd insisted on stopping to see her mother on their way to Michigan. His heart had nearly stopped when that headline linked the sniper victim with the massacre, and it had been all he could do to cover.

They were on the right track. He knew it.

So why the hell were they diddling around now?

"My putting myself in the spotlight has made Mom worry about me," Renata said. "I want her to see me, to know I'm okay, so that if she can't reach me..."

Trying to empathize, Gabe hadn't argued. A small delay was nothing, he'd told himself, not after all this time. So he'd simply followed Renata's directions and had taken Lake Shore Drive south of the Loop to the Kenwood neighborhood, down a tree-lined street to the century-old graystone two-flat where her mom lived.

"Let's just play it casual," Renata said as they climbed the stairs.

"Casual, it is."

They entered a vestibule with two doors. Renata rang one of the bells, and mere seconds later, the first-floor door was opened by a woman who looked nothing like Renata. Her hair and eyes were fair and she was shorter and more well-rounded. But upon seeing Renata, her face lit up and Gabe had no doubts as to who she was.

"Sweetheart, I've been so worried about you."

Renata hugged the woman and kissed her cheek. "I told you everything would be all right."

"And who is this young man?"

"Gabriel Connor," Gabe said and, extra-casually, added, "A friend."

Mrs. Fox's eyebrows shot up. "I see. Come in."

"Just for a minute," Renata said. "Then we have to leave."

"Why the rush?"

Renata met Gabe's gaze and said, "We're on our way to Michigan, and I just wanted to stop by for a moment."

"Oh." Soft color brushed Mrs. Fox's cheeks and she gave Gabe a more appraising look.

Renata quickly added, "We won't be back until really late tonight. I just figured you might worry if you couldn't get hold of me again. So before we left, I just wanted you to see me in person for yourself. I know how worried you've been with all the media attention."

"It just reminds me of—"

"I know, Mom." Renata gave her mother a big hug.

And Gabe gave them a moment.

He wandered farther into the living room, which looked as if it had been decorated a few decades ago and had never been updated. He stopped before a curio cabinet whose top shelf held a photo of a man in uniform. Renata's father, no doubt about it. He looked even more Native American than her. And in addition to the portrait, there were a couple of medals. And a framed newspaper clipping—his casket being carried by other policemen in dress uniform and a headline that screamed that another cop had been killed on the job.

Obviously, after all these years, Mrs. Fox was still mourning her late husband. And Renata was trying to reassure her mother that the same thing wouldn't happen to her. As if she could be sure of anything herself, considering the things that had happened in the past several days.

"Well, don't rush back," Mrs. Fox was saying. "You deserve some time off. You two have fun."

"My middle name," Gabe assured her with a wink.

They headed back for the car, and Renata's mother stood in the doorway, watching until they pulled away.

Considering Renata was so up front most of the time, Gabe couldn't quite get what had just happened. "Do you really think dishonesty protects your mother?"

"I didn't lie."

"No, you just led her to believe you and I were going away to play. She thinks we're—"

"I know what she thinks. She made an assumption and I simply didn't bother to correct her."

"You let her think what you wanted her to think," Gabe said. "What you planned on her thinking before we ever walked into the house."

"All right. I admit it. Mom had a really hard time after Dad died. I guess you'd call it a nervous breakdown. She wouldn't even go out of the house for months, unless it was to visit his grave. It's really hard sometimes, knowing the right thing to do. I believed in Dad, in his wanting to make the city safer. And I always wanted to follow in his footsteps. I tried not to for a while—for Mom's sake—but I felt I wasn't being true to myself."

"And to your dad."

"And to my dad," she admitted. "I have to do this, Gabe. And not just because someone is after me, though that is a great motivator. I have to do this for my family—Mom and my sister Lucille."

Gabe saw Renata's choices as her trying to protect her mother while living her life for her father. A real juggling act. Whether or not she wanted to admit it, she was trying to make up for what had happened to her dad, as if she could clear his name by doing

well on the job herself. Somehow she must think that
once she did that, her mom and her sister and she
would be okay.

Not necessarily, as he knew from experience.

No matter how hard you tried, you couldn't fix the
past. And sometimes you couldn't even forget it. It
followed you around like a dark shadow, waiting
until you're at your most vulnerable…

But he knew she had to try.

Gabe could identify with the family entangle-
ment. That was something they had in common and
another reason to feel close to her.

Trouble was, he was feeling a little too close for
his own comfort.

POSSIBILITIES ABOUT what might happen next ran
through Renata's mind from all directions, but no answers came to her. She was running on empty, her
mind exhausted by the friction at work, the media attention and trying to keep her mom from pitching
over the edge again.

And then there was Gabriel Connor. Or whatever
his real name was. Rather, her growing feelings for
him. What the heck was she going to do about them?

The attraction might be mutual, but she wasn't
foolish enough to get crazy romantic ideas. Nothing
romantic about this situation at all. They were simply two people drawn together by uncertainty and
danger. She imagined when this was all over, they
probably would never see each other again.

An unsettling thought, one she didn't want to

probe into more deeply, any more than she wanted to probe into Gabe's true identity.

Renata didn't know why, but Ned Coulter's asking if he was still using the name Gabriel Connor had shocked her. Knowing he had his own agenda and hadn't been totally up front with her, she should have been prepared for another curve. But she hadn't been prepared for that.

There'd been that moment between them when she'd wanted to ask…but she'd let it pass.

Gabe wasn't volunteering any more information about himself, and Renata simply couldn't ask him. Her greatest fear was that if she knew who he was— someone with a record?—she would have to walk away. And then she would be alone in this.

Finding the truth about the City Sniper, about who was trying to kill her, was challenge enough. She was juggling too much now and didn't know how to make sense of things. Or even to slow down. This thing had built a life of its own and she was simply following where it led them.

Currently to Michigan, she thought, forcing away a sudden yearning to be in Gabe's arms.

She checked her watch. They'd been on the road about an hour and a half, so they were more than halfway to Embry Lake, one of many small lake towns in southwestern Michigan, and she still didn't know exactly what she could or would do when they got there.

"We'll have to start with Leigh Ann Ackerman," she mused, forcing herself to concentrate on the only thing she did know for sure. "The 'widow' has been making waves ever since the standoff at Embry Lake." Even though she hadn't been part of S.A.F.E. when it had happened, she preferred thinking of the Embry Lake incident that way—a standoff rather than a massacre. Things had somehow gotten out of hand, though, and civilians had been the ones to die. "She got herself a top lawyer who's demanding millions of dollars for the survivors."

"Hmm. Do you think she really believes her husband is dead?" Gabe asked. "Rather, that he was killed in the standoff?"

"I don't know. Unless he had reason to want out of the marriage. Though why he wouldn't simply divorce her…" The name switch kept bugging her, though. "Why would Russell Ackerman have felt it necessary to change his name?"

"He was afraid someone would put a bullet in him?" Gabe offered.

She didn't miss the irony of the man's fate. "But why? Who?"

"If he was in on a scam with his wife, maybe someone who didn't want to pay up," Gabe said. "More likely, it was someone who didn't like the fact that he ran out on his militia compatriots."

"But Joshua Hague was already dead." As far as Renata knew, he would have been the one to fear. "Who else?"

"If we answer that question correctly, we win a new washer and dryer and the identity of a murderer."

Gabe injected humor at the strangest times. Another *why*. What had happened to him to make him so flippant about serious matters? His way of dealing with them, she supposed, though he hadn't been flippant earlier, when they'd first found the information.

"Let's hope Leigh Ann Ackerman has some answers," she muttered.

THE AIR FELT thick and Gabe was having a hard time breathing by the time they arrived in Embry Lake. Gabe's need for the truth and justice was becoming more urgent with time.

He pulled into a gas station and stopped at a pump.

"We need gas," he told Renata. "See if you can get directions to the widow's place."

"Yes, sir!"

He met her gaze, which held a shadow of that curiosity that had him worried. She hadn't asked about his real name or why he'd had to change it. He hadn't had to lie.

He wanted to keep things that way.

They both got out of the car and stretched. And while Renata went inside to find someone who could give them directions, Gabe opened the tank, swiped his credit card and started filling up.

Gideon had put him on to Ned Coulter. When he'd originally hit town, the club owner had used the identification specialist to help him create a new persona. Gabe had done the same, not because he'd absolutely had to—not like Gideon—but because change had become a habit that was difficult to break. If you didn't settle down in one place, didn't keep the same name, you couldn't be found by someone who could hurt you…who could possibly be the death of you.

He'd learned that mantra the hard way, and he couldn't shake it and relax.

Not even now.

Thinking about the past made him want to call his own mother, just to hear her voice. And to tell her he was finally going to get justice for Danny. But he couldn't do that to her. She would know. And then she would be frantic for him, just like Renata's mother was for her.

Yeah, the one thing they had in common…

Renata came out of the station with arms and hands full. "I got the directions. The Ackerman place is about two miles out of town around the southern end of the lake."

"Good." He indicated the load she was carrying. "What did you do? Buy out the store?"

"I was hungry and wanted to make sure we had everything we needed. And that doesn't make me obsessive-compulsive," she informed him.

Grinning that she'd beat him to saying it, he told her, "I like a woman with healthy appetites."

"I think you've mentioned that before," she muttered, setting the drinks on the roof so she could open the passenger door.

The tank was full, so Gabe took his receipt and

pulled the car over to the side of the station where they immediately wolfed down the fast food—hot dogs, French fries and nachos with a potato-chip chaser.

Mouth full, he joked, "You didn't buy antacids for dessert, did you?"

"Fried pies," she said, waving the packages at him.

Fast food or not, Gabe felt better after eating. A little more relaxed, less suffocated. Definitely ready to face whatever was ahead of them.

The drive was barely five minutes and by the time they pulled up at the white-sided building sitting across from the lake, Gabe felt the tension building once more.

"Well, this is it, then," he murmured.

Renata said, "Let's hope so. We're due for a break. And justice needs to be served."

Indeed it did, Gabe thought, following her to the house. Only he knew his definition of justice would be different from hers.

The thing that would ultimately keep them apart...

LEIGH ANN ACKERMAN looked to be in her late twenties. There was nothing soft about her, Renata thought, as they sat in the living room. No frills, either in her person or in the plain contemporary furnishings. Leigh Ann herself had short dark hair and no makeup, and wore loose denim overalls over a long-sleeved blue Henley. Even so, she couldn't hide the fact that she was a naturally beautiful woman. And pregnant.

Renata and Gabe sat, while Leigh Ann stood over them, arms crossed.

"Are you here to make a settlement offer?" she asked.

Renata had simply told the woman they represented S.A.F.E.—a general statement in hopes that she wouldn't look too closely at Gabe's presence.

"I'm afraid not," Renata said. "I'm here to ask you some questions about your husband, Russell Ackerman."

"My late husband."

"Yes, he is dead now."

Leigh Ann frowned. "What does that mean?"

"He didn't die here at Embry Lake as reported. The body in the fire was misidentified."

The widow groped for the chair behind her and sat. "Y-you're lying."

"Am I? To what point?"

"You want me to drop the suit against S.A.F.E. You can't intimidate me."

"We're not concerned about the suit," Gabe said. "We're trying to get to the truth of why your husband would pretend to be dead."

Leigh Ann gaped at him, then said, "If you think *I* know anything about this…"

"So you didn't know he was living in Chicago under an assumed name?" Renata asked.

"Assumed… No, I don't believe it! You're saying he's alive?"

Renata swore the surprise in the woman's voice was real. And, perhaps, the hope. Perhaps she really didn't know anything about Russell Ackerman's activities. He had been part of the Embry Lake Brigade, after all. Militia men weren't the most open about their activities.

Renata dug into her shoulder bag and pulled out the envelope she'd picked up at S.A.F.E. "I have a photograph here that I would like you to look at." She flipped it around and asked, "Do you recognize this man?"

"Th-that's Russell."

"It's also Chuck LaRoe," Renata said, satisfied they had the right man. She put the photo away. "Russell Ackerman left Michigan and moved to Chicago, but he was murdered two weeks ago. If you keep abreast of the news, surely you heard about the City Sniper who was killing Chicago residents and—"

"Murdered? Russell? He's been killed again?"

Leigh Ann choked back a sound of horror, but she couldn't stop the tears from coming. She cried in true grief fashion, alternately gasping for air and wailing. Just as Renata's mom had when her dad had been killed. And for months afterward.

She met Gabe's gaze. What now? It didn't seem as though the widow knew anything.

"We're sorry for your loss," Gabe said, his voice neutral, "but we need to ask you some questions."

The widow ignored the condolences and continued wailing so loud that Renata didn't hear the door opening.

"What the hell's going on here?" A tall, thin man

whose brown hair was streaked with gray stormed into the gathering and went directly to Leigh Ann's side. "Hey, what did they do to you?"

Leigh Ann shook her head and kept crying.

"We brought her some bad news," Gabe said. "Her husband's dead."

"She's known that for more'n six months."

"Actually, he died about two weeks ago," Renata corrected him. "Russell Ackerman didn't die in the fire, as was surmised. He was shot to death in Chicago two weeks ago."

The man didn't say anything but Renata noted the subtle shift in his features, as if this all wasn't exactly news to him. Then he focused on Leigh Ann.

"Can I get you something? Tea, maybe?"

Leigh Ann nodded and tried to get hold of herself.

And the man turned to them. "You'll have to leave now," he said flatly. "Your upsetting her isn't good for the baby."

Wondering who he was, Renata asked, "And you are…?"

"Hank Oeland. The man who's going to call the sheriff and report a couple of trespassers if you don't get out now. No one around here likes you people."

"You don't even know who we are."

"Feds," the man spat. "You got the smell on you. Unless you got a warrant?"

"We'll leave," Renata said, rising and signaling Gabe to do the same.

She'd hated bringing Ackerman's widow the bad news. And the last thing in the world she wanted was to continue an unproductive confrontation that would upset Leigh Ann further. Not to mention that it would get straight back to Mulvihill.

As they left the house, she noticed a black truck parked on the other side of the street. Wondering where Oeland had parked his vehicle, she nudged Gabe. "Do you think that could be Oeland's?" she asked.

"It wasn't there when we went inside. Still, there are plenty of black trucks in Michigan. The one that followed us didn't have any kind of markings that we could see."

But they paused, staring, long enough that sounds of Leigh Ann Ackerman crying like her heart had been broken drifted out to them. Getting into Gabe's car, Renata wondered what it felt like to love a man so deeply. Her only other experience was also one of the observer—her mom had never recovered from her dad's death.

Renata glanced at Gabe and felt warmth rush through her as she remembered the moment's panic she'd experienced when she'd thought he was hurt in Chinatown. But that was because she'd brought him into the situation and felt responsible. And yes, she had some kind of mixed-up feelings for him, though she didn't want to put a name to them.

She'd never been in love herself, and she wasn't about to let emotions distract her now.

Chapter Eleven

"So what next?" Gabe asked as they perused their dinner menus.

After leaving Russell Ackerman's widow, they'd driven to the compound, the scene of the massacre, but the place had been locked up tight. It had looked deserted to Gabe.

Then they'd spent a couple of hours trying to pick up Russell Ackerman's trail, but everyone who'd known the man had seemed as surprised as the widow that he'd gotten out of the massacre alive. Of course they hadn't questioned everyone in town. Yet.

When his stomach had screamed for mercy, Gabe had staged a one-man revolt and insisted they hit one of the local eateries. So here they were in what had turned out to be a nice little restaurant across from the lake.

A decent menu, low lights, a wood-burning fireplace…Gabe flicked his gaze to Renata and wondered what having dinner with her would be like under different circumstances.

She set down her menu and said, "We could keep prodding people until there's no one left to prod, but my best guess is it won't do any good. So when we're done eating, we might as well head for home."

Gabe didn't blame her for being discouraged. She'd had such high hopes that the discovery of Chuck LaRoe's true identity was going to lead them somewhere. That maybe the puzzle would start unraveling.

"Did you buy Leigh Ann's grief?" he asked as the waitress stopped to fill their coffee cups.

Renata seemed surprised. "Didn't you?"

"It kind of pre-empted our asking too many questions about Russell Ackerman."

"The woman just learned she lost the same husband twice. How else was she supposed to respond?"

The waitress gave a little "Hmph," and then asked, "Decided yet?" Her penciled eyebrows raised all the way into her blond bangs.

Gabe studied her expression as he said, "Excuse me…" He glanced at her name tag. "…Carol…"

"Your food order," she clarified.

"I mean the first part. You made that little noise of disapproval."

Suddenly seeming uncomfortable, she said, "Oh, it was nothing. I shouldn't be listening in to customers' conversations. But it's like, well, hard to avoid sometimes."

"Perhaps you were making an observation about Leigh Ann Ackerman?" he persisted.

At first, Gabe didn't think she would answer, but

then he saw the indecision in her features. Undoubtedly she was wondering about their interest in the local woman.

"She's not in trouble or anything," he assured her. "We simply delivered some bad news about her husband and she broke up pretty bad."

"Hmph." The waitress appeared disbelieving. "If she loved Russell so much, Leigh Ann sure didn't wait long to find herself another man and get herself pregnant by him."

"Russell Ackerman isn't the father of the baby?" Renata asked.

"She tries to say it is, but does that woman look seven or eight months' pregnant to you?" the waitress asked Renata.

"I don't know," Renata said. "I didn't think about it."

Carol went on. "Some folks say Hank Oeland had a thing for her even while she was married to Russell. Maybe the feeling was mutual."

"Are you trying to tell us that she didn't love her husband?" Gabe asked.

"Well, no… I mean, I don't really know. They were having lots of problems. You could hear the fights just walking along the lake. She hated his belonging to the Brigade. Weird thing is, Hank belongs, too."

"What does this Hank Oeland look like?" Gabe asked.

"Tall, thin, brown hair with some gray in it."

The man who'd thrown them out of the house. Gabe exchanged a meaningful look with Renata.

"So, are you ready to order or what?"

Gabe turned back to the waitress and smiled at her. "And what would you recommend, Carol?"

"The rib eye is great. Real tender."

The rib eye steak was also the most expensive thing on the menu. "Two rib eyes it is, then."

When Renata seemed about to protest, he stopped her with a frown. She frowned back but waited until the waitress left to put in their order.

"What if I don't want red meat?" she asked.

"Then stick to the rabbit food that comes with it and I'll eat the steak. Carol's been very forthcoming. Let's keep her in a good mood in case we need more information later."

"Your mind works in mysterious ways."

"I have my methods," he said, taking a slug of coffee. "So what about the local gossip?"

"The Hank Oeland thing? I don't know how much truth to that there is. Leigh Ann really didn't take the news about her husband well," Renata mused.

"Maybe she knew Ackerman didn't die in the fire but didn't know about the sniper, either. Maybe she thought he was still alive."

Renata shook her head. "I don't think so. I think she just loved him too much. Which makes it odd that she would get involved with another man so quickly. Maybe she really isn't involved with Oeland. Maybe it *is* just small town gossip."

Loved him too much...

Gabe didn't know there could be too much love in the world and he wondered why Renata thought so.

"But what if it isn't gossip?" he said. "She is pregnant. According to Carol, she's not big enough to have been with child before the standoff."

"Maybe. But one of my cousins was due any day and still wearing regular clothes only a size bigger than normal. So size doesn't necessarily tell the whole story."

"Let's play 'what if,'" Gabe said, looking around to make certain no one was close enough to hear. Even so, he lowered his voice. "Carol said Oeland was in love with Leigh Ann before the standoff. What if that's true?" Wondering what he might go through for a woman he loved, Gabe suspected whatever was necessary. When he realized he was staring at Renata, he quickly added, "What if Oeland knew that Ackerman survived? What if he didn't want Ackerman to reunite with his wife?"

"You mean you think Oeland hired the sharpshooter?" Renata asked in a conspiratorial whisper.

"What if Oeland *is* the sharpshooter? He is part of a local militia. Who knows what he's trained to do?"

Though Renata seemed to have lost her breath at that suggestion, she said, "But how would he have known where to find someone in hiding under an assumed name?"

"They were both members of the Brigade. There could have been other plans afoot and the two men might have been communicating."

"All right," she agreed. "All that is something to consider. Oeland a sharpshooter. If we plugged his name into a search engine, I wonder if we would find connections with any of the victims or people related or connected to them."

"Let's find out as soon as we can get our hands on a computer," he said, then noticed the waitress coming toward them, salads in hand. "Ah, food. Good."

With a waitress who admitted to habitual fascination with customer conversations nearby, they would just have to hold off on anything they didn't want spread around town. They would have plenty of time to go over everything they knew about the case on the three-hour ride back to Chicago.

"So what about you?" Gabe asked as they ate their salads. "What do you have against love?"

Renata started and protested, "I don't have anything against love."

"Ever been married or engaged?"

"No, but—"

"How about a serious relationship?"

"Where is this coming from?" she asked.

"I thought not."

"Gabe—"

"Your comment about loving too much. It hit me that you were a little soured on love."

Renata put down her fork and pushed her salad away. "Okay, if you're wondering if I had some tragic love affair…no. But what happened to my mom after my dad died…"

"Are you anything like your mother?"

"Not really."

"Then why would you be afraid to take a chance on love?"

"Why would *you* be?" she countered, turning the tables on him. "Have you ever been married or engaged, and if not, why not?"

"Maybe I've never stayed in one place long enough to find a special someone."

Even as he said it, he thought about how special Renata was. Beautiful and intelligent in addition to being the most honest and upright and focused woman he'd ever met.

"What?" she murmured, her lips delectable and oh so tempting. "Are you telling me the romantic doesn't believe in love at first sight?"

"I believe in lust at first sight."

Gabe purposely intensified his stare and was rewarded with a blush darkening Renata's cheeks.

He *was* in lust with her, had been from the moment he'd laid eyes on her. But for some reason, lust didn't cover it any more. Lust was what happened between the sheets. And what he was feeling permeated every moment he was with her. And some moments when he wasn't, as well.

Just thinking about getting more personal with Renata set off alarms. It would never work between them, not when he was using her to get at Mulvihill.

Once she figured that out, they would be history.

So what in the world had gotten into Gabe with all that love talk? Renata wondered as they left the restaurant and walked into a fog that rose from the lake and spread its tentacles all around. Though she was trying to be cool about it, her discomfort still hadn't completely dissipated.

But when Gabe asked, "Where's the car?" she was jolted out of her self-absorbed mood.

"The car?"

She peered through the haze at the vehicles in the lot. Not many left. None of them Gabe's.

His curse was low and vehement. "I can't believe this. Someone stole my damn car!"

Renata didn't argue. What other explanation was there? "But who stole it and why?" she murmured.

"Just because we're not in the big city doesn't mean there are no thieves around."

"So you think it's coincidence?" Renata asked. "I don't believe in them."

Gabe seemed to mull that over for a moment. "Oeland?" he finally said. "To what purpose?"

"To slow us down, I suppose."

She only hoped that was all Hank Oeland—if he, indeed, was the thief—had in mind.

The next hour was filled with making out a police report, calling Gabe's insurance company and learning that, unless they walked, they wouldn't be able to get out of town until midmorning. That's when the only bus came through. They could then get to a city, where they could rent a car.

The deputy was nice enough to drop them off at a motel where they would be forced to spend the night.

"Okay, the Bates Motel had nothing on this place," Gabe said.

"It's just the fog," Renata said, trying to convince him as well as herself. The place was run-down-looking; its most attractive feature was the blinking red neon sign—Water's Edge Cabins, Vacancy. "The fog is spooky."

"We're sticking together," Gabe told her as they approached the office.

Her pulse picked up and she asked, "To what purpose?"

"Safety in numbers."

Indeed, if the killer were around and responsible for Gabe's car doing a disappearing act, Renata didn't want to be alone.

She peered into the fog as if she could actually see someone staring back. Her skin crawled and the hair at the back of her neck stood at attention and she cursed herself for being so gullible before following Gabe inside.

Even though she knew her imagination was working overtime, she didn't argue about the accommodations. She let him handle it, knowing she would feel more secure in his company.

Safer in his arms.

She shook off the image that thought brought with it.

A few minutes later, they were in the "cabin" they would call home for the night.

"Charming," Renata murmured.

Cabin was a misnomer. It was simply a single room with a kitchenette. While the place looked as if it had been recently cleaned, the carpeting was stained and the curtains and spread looked old and dull. She hadn't expected much in the way of amenities—good thing, because there were none. No table. No chairs. Only a bed.

Her stomach dropped when she took a second look—it was a full-sized bed, barely big enough for two adults.

It was going to be a long night.

"At least the heat's on and it's nice and cozy," Gabe said. "You want to hit the shower first?"

"Why bother? I'm just going to sleep in my clothes."

"Only if you want to. It's okay with me if you take them all off."

She just bet it would be. "I'll take off my jacket and my shoes. And my gun."

"Thanks for that. I've never been comfortable sleeping with a gun in the bed."

"You make it sound like you've done it."

"Not for years."

Somehow, she didn't think he was kidding. "Why?"

"I was always afraid my father was going to catch up with us."

Renata stared. She'd expected him to make a joke of it. Instead, he'd given her an unexpected insight into his past.

"Your father was violent?"

"Especially to my mother. But to me, too, if I stepped between them. And sometimes just for fun."

"Gabe—"

"Forget it. That was a long time ago. Another lifetime. And don't worry, I no longer carry a gun. I don't want to be anything like my father. And I shouldn't have said anything."

"I'm sorry."

"Well, that makes two of us."

Another lifetime…another name? Is that why Gabe knew Ned Coulter? Because he needed to stay hidden from a violent father? But that didn't make sense, considering he was an adult. What could his father do to him now?

"So where does your mother call home these days?"

"At the moment, she's in Milwaukee. But I'm hoping that someday soon, she'll feel comfortable enough to move to Chicago so I can see her more often."

Which sounded like he was in Chicago to stay, Renata thought, realizing the idea gave her a sense of well-being she couldn't explain.

She removed her shoes and jacket, then stripped off her holster. Trying not to notice how much clothing Gabe was removing, she kept her back to him, then tried to lie at the edge of the bed. Unfortunately, her body kept wanting to roll toward the sagging middle. She tried different positions and finally found that if she stayed on her right side, she could drop her left arm over and cling to the edge of the mattress.

"Can I turn out the lights?" Gabe asked.

"Go ahead. We both need to get some sleep if we want to be functional in the morning."

Apparently Gabe was serious about taking that shower, because a few seconds after the light went off, she heard the bathroom door swing shut. And after that, screeching pipes and the flow of running water. Outside their door, lake water lapped against the dock. All of the sounds melded together and the tension of the day drained from her. Renata felt herself slipping away.

Exhausted, she let herself drift...

Sometime later, an oppressive heat woke her. She stirred, then realized she couldn't move. Another body spooned her, an arm held her captive.

Her eyes flashed open. Gabe!

He was like a furnace—she was so warm she could hardly breathe—and he was asleep if the sounds he was making were any indication. Well, not all of him was asleep. He was hard against her. Literally. She could feel his erection solid and long against her backside.

Her mouth went dry and her heart skipped a beat. Unable to help herself, she pressed back against him and slowly moved her hips. He made an agonized sound in his sleep and his hand moved up her belly to find a breast under her sweater. The touch lit an instant fire in her. Her body came alive, demanding she take care of it. Even as she fought with herself mentally, she couldn't stop herself from moving against him, imagining what it would be like to feel him inside her.

This wasn't rational, Renata told herself. She couldn't get too involved with Gabe. She needed to concentrate on this case for both their sakes. Sex would only complicate things between them.

But her body wasn't listening.

"Gabe," she whispered in protest.

But he wasn't listening, either.

Stirring, obviously finding he wasn't just having an erotic dream, he slipped his fingers inside her bra and his breath sent a trail of gooseflesh along her neck. Her resolve melted away like ice under a bright sun.

That's what Gabe felt like…a bright sun…. Renata had never been so hot.

She turned in his arms and faced him as his eyes flickered open. She read surprise along with desire. He was just waking up. It didn't take him long to get in rhythm with her thoughts. Closing his eyes again, he covered her mouth with his and plunged his tongue inside. She closed her eyes, too, and savored the sensations.

His hands were all over her now, smoothing and teasing. They wrapped around her back and she felt the constraint around her chest lift as he undid her bra. Then his hands cupped her breasts, his fingers found her nipples, and a pleasurable sensation spread through her and intensified until she needed to touch him in return.

Her hands dipped down his washboard abs, finding his quickening flesh through his briefs. He groaned her name against her mouth.

She was so hot she couldn't stand it.

When she plunged both hands down along his

skin inside the material, he came alive. Her fingers surrounded him, and he filled her hand.

Imagining him filling her in other places, she could hardly get her breath.

Hot…she was so hot…couldn't get hotter.

But when he got into her pants, his fingers cleverly spreading her and dipping inside her, sliding in with ease along the wet, slippery path, she did get hotter.

He stroked her and she helped him, angling her hips so he could deepen the thrust of his fingers. But it wasn't his fingers she wanted to pleasure her.

Opening her mouth to tell him what she did want, she felt a burning sensation at the back of her throat and coughed instead. Suddenly, she realized how hard it was to breathe. And why. Rather than air, smoke filled her lungs.

She flashed her eyes open and realized the room was thick with smoke.

"Fire!" she choked out.

"You're on fire, all right."

"No, the room!"

Opening his eyes, Gabe swore and let go of her. "We've got to get out of here."

They both rolled off the mattress in opposite directions, he pulling on his pants, she finding her shoes as she got to her feet. She felt for her holster and slung it on.

"Come on!" he urged her. "No time."

As they moved across the room, she slipped into her jacket. But the smoke was billowing in from under the door, as if the porch were on fire.

"Can't go that way," Gabe said.

"The roof is on fire!" Smoke and cinders were descending on them and she saw a flame in one corner. "There's no back door. We'll never get out of here alive!"

Inhaling too much smoke, she started coughing.

"Then a window."

Gabe grabbed the bed covers and dragged her into the bathroom and turned on the shower.

"What are you doing?" she coughed out.

"Wetting the bedding."

He held the spread, blanket and sheet under the spray, then quickly opened the bathroom window. Smoke immediately filled the small space. Renata futilely tried to hold her breath but the coughing intensified.

"Okay, bad idea," he said, coughing, as well, and slammed the window shut.

It didn't matter, she continued to cough, frozen to the spot, until Gabe propelled her back into the other room.

"We have to go out the front way," he said, heaving the wet bedding over them before hooking an arm around her waist. "Ready?"

She coughed in response. She couldn't stop coughing. Couldn't move. Even though she was tented against the smoke, it had already gotten to her. The room started whirling around her and her legs felt like they were ready to collapse.

Gabe steadied her and swept her forward, saying, "Get ready to run like hell."

She heard the last in a vacuum. Woozy, she tripped over her own feet and would have fallen to the floor if not for Gabe, who picked her up.

"Hang on to my neck!"

Renata managed to get her arms up as Gabe grabbed for the door. He threw it open and plunged head first through smoke and flames so fast that Renata felt as if she were flying.

And then she realized she *was* flying—they both were—as the freezing lake water came up to greet them.

Chapter Twelve

With a burst of flames and a shriek of tearing wood, the roof collapsed, disappearing inside the burning walls.

They'd made it out just in time, Gabe thought, as he got to his feet in thigh-high water and realized other people, most dressed in nightclothes, were running their way to see what was going on.

Renata, still clinging to him and coughing, was trying to stand, as well.

"Are you all right?" he asked, helping her. "Don't try to talk, just nod or something."

She nodded and gasped. "Fine," she gritted out, the sound hoarse and raspy. "Thanks to you."

"Let's get to dry land."

He felt her shiver against him and pulled her closer. They were both wet and the night was cold. He heard shouts and realized people were running to help them. Several had dry blankets they piled onto the two of them. Even so, he looked around at the dozen or so people surrounding them and wondered if one of them was the arsonist.

There was no doubt in his mind that the blaze had been purposely set.

That someone wanted them dead was no big surprise, not after the truck incident. So did that truck belong to Hank Oeland? Had Oeland felt threatened and come after them on his own turf? Or did they have an invisible enemy that even he couldn't fathom? Gabe wondered.

A siren split the night, followed by the sound of emergency vehicles arriving. It had taken the fire department long enough, but Gabe supposed in a town this size, the team was made up of volunteers.

"The killer is here," Renata rasped out, her mind apparently in tandem with his.

They *were* in tandem in so many ways, Gabe thought, pulling her closer and flagging down the ambulance that showed up just before the fire truck.

The next half hour was filled with noise and confusion. As men doused the fire, paramedics checked him and Renata over. They decided he was fine but that Renata needed to take a trip to the emergency room so she could be more thoroughly checked out by a doctor.

"Sir, you'll have to take your own car. You can't ride in the ambulance," one of the paramedics told him as they got Renata inside.

"Someone stole my car. And try to stop me."

Gabe climbed in after Renata. He wasn't about to leave her alone.

Who knew if the killer lurked nearby, just waiting to finish the job on her?

The paramedic looked as if he wanted to argue, but after meeting Gabe's cold stare, he looked away and shut the doors. The fifteen-minute ride to the closest hospital felt like an eternity. He held Renata's hand all the way there and wanted to protest when they placed her in a cubicle where they would further examine her and asked him to wait down the hall. Knowing they would work faster without him around to get in the way, he went quietly.

After being given a pair of scrubs to replace his clothes until they dried, Gabe paced the halls of the hospital while waiting for an update on Renata. When word came a half hour later—that she seemed to be fine other than having a raw throat, that the medical staff merely wanted to keep her for observation for several hours—he was shocked at the depth of his relief.

Of course, he wouldn't want *anyone* to be hurt so recklessly, but, despite himself, he had extra care for the woman he'd grown so close to in a matter of days. The woman he'd almost made love to barely two hours before.

When he was allowed in to see her, Renata was sitting up in bed. She was dressed in a shapeless hospital gown, her face was stripped clean not only of soot but of any makeup, and her hair was still crusted with soot. And Gabe thought he'd never seen anything more beautiful.

"They tell me you'll live," he joked, disappointed when he didn't get a smile out of her.

"So it seems. That was a close one."

From her dour expression to her fingers plucking at the sheet, he figured she was blaming herself for not being watchful enough.

He sat next to her on the bed and said, "Too close," then placed his hand over hers to reassure her. "But neither of us is to blame, Renata. The killer might be right behind us, but we don't even know who to look for. We just have to watch each other's backs."

"You *did* watch mine." Her soulful gaze met his. "You saved my life."

She looked so serious, he wanted to kiss away her frown. But he dared not. He shouldn't even be touching her. Or sitting so close.

"I guess we're even, then," he said with a shrug far more casual than he was feeling, "which is good, because I don't like owing a debt that big."

Renata did smile then, and Gabe's heart thumped against his ribs as if he'd been exerting himself. A warmth spread through him, warning him that he was in big trouble.

Heart trouble.

Uh-oh...

Damn if he hadn't gone and fallen for a government agent!

SOME NICE SOUL in the hospital laundry had dried their things. Renata was appreciative. She hadn't looked forward to dressing in damp clothes. Nor had she looked forward to taking public transportation or getting to some place to rent a car to get home.

Now they didn't have to.

The Embry Lake authorities had shown up earlier, and not only had they taken her and Gabe's statements, but they'd returned Gabe's car. It seemed that whoever had stolen it had abandoned it within sight of the motel office. So they'd had it dusted for fingerprints and then one of the deputies had driven it to the hospital.

Renata signed the release papers and a nurse wheeled her to a hospital door, where Gabe took over.

"You don't need to help me," she protested in a hoarse voice, though as usual, he didn't listen to her.

As he guided her to the car, his hands were all over her, reminding her of what had almost happened between them. She got a quick flash of the way he'd looked when they'd almost made love… followed immediately by a flash of the fire.

Thankfully, the torture was short-lived and they were on their way.

And thankfully, Gabe didn't insist on keeping up a conversation. No doubt he was trying to be thoughtful of her throat. She simply was too distracted with her own thoughts about the case—about their almost dying—to engage in the banter he seemed to savor.

The closer they got to Chicago, the more sure she was of what she had to do.

Pulse humming, knowing Gabe wasn't going to like her plans for the afternoon, she said, "When we get back in the city, take me to my place."

"You think that's wise?"

"I think it's necessary. I need to clean up and put on fresh clothes before going into the office."

"Office?"

He sounded shocked, Renata realized. No doubt he figured she should keep her distance from all things S.A.F.E. for as long as possible.

"As much as I hate having to do it," she admitted, "I need to talk to Mulvihill."

"Don't."

Startled by his vehemence, she said, "I have to, Gabe. Mulvihill has to know about the Embry Lake connection."

"If he believes you."

"I have to take that chance."

"You're going to put yourself in more danger."

"You don't know that." And why he thought that puzzled her. She might be putting her job in more danger, but not herself. Even so… "I get paid to be in danger, you don't. I almost got you killed. Again."

"It wasn't your fault. You didn't do anything wrong."

"I've probably done *everything* wrong, even though my intentions were the best."

Her voice was going, so Renata took a sip of the water she'd brought along with her to soothe her throat. She wasn't working on impulse; while waiting to be released from the hospital, she'd had plenty of time to think about how to proceed.

"This is a S.A.F.E. matter," she said, "and I'm going to try throwing it back at the agency and see if it sticks this time. Maybe with this new information…"

Embry Lake had been a disaster for S.A.F.E. and now there was a connection between the massacre and the City Sniper shootings. At least one of them. She couldn't not hand over that information. Surely, Elliott Mulvihill would have to act on this report.

"What if it doesn't stick?" Gabe asked, his tone terse.

"Then I'm back where I started—"

Before she could say "alone," Gabe cut in. "You mean *we're* back where *we* started."

"No, Gabe."

"Promise me, Renata. Or I'll run with it myself. With other members of the team."

She knew he wasn't bluffing. The thing she still didn't know was why.

"Why, Gabe? Why is this so important to you?"

"You're important to me. No matter what you say, I'm not going to leave you to hang out to dry alone."

She didn't want to continue the argument. Her emotions were suddenly feeling as raw as her throat. But Gabe wouldn't leave it alone.

"You do realize this means Mulvihill will shut you down."

"He already did that."

"Then why are you going back for more?"

"Because it's my job. It's who I am."

"You're not your job. You're so much more than your job. You're one of the best people I've ever met. And I'm only getting to know you."

Though she was appreciative of the compliment, she didn't pursue that line of thought. And as if he'd realized he couldn't do anything to change her mind, Gabe ceased trying to do so. With the steering wheel in what looked like a death grip, he stared at the road ahead.

Renata felt his anger, though. It washed over her in waves and made her sick inside. She didn't want to be at odds with Gabe over this. She also didn't want him to risk his life for her again. She didn't want anyone to die for her, but especially not him.

Not when she'd just found him…

SEVERAL HOURS LATER, Renata was at her computer, trying to put thoughts of Gabe on hold.

Even though it was a Saturday, the office was at half staff, agents working on current cases. Even Mulvihill was in his office. She was making out another report—detailing information about Chuck LaRoe/Russell Ackerman, Hank Oeland and the fire that had almost ended her investigation—when Paul Broden stuck his head inside her cubicle.

"Hey, back to work already? I thought you were on orders to stay away until summoned."

Saving the document, she said, "New developments."

"Really." He stepped inside and perched at the edge of her desk. "Something viable?"

"One of the victims was using an assumed identity."

He frowned. "What's with the voice?"

"I'm allergic to smoke." Actually, her throat was feeling better and she was sounding a little more normal than earlier. She set up the document to print. "Chuck LaRoe's real name was Russell Ackerman."

"Ackerman. That's familiar."

"Embry Lake."

"What?" Broden's shock was palpable.

"He supposedly died there."

"Are you sure about this?"

"Positive."

Broden mumbled a curse and said, "You may have hit on something. Not that Mulvihill will want to hear it."

Renata met his gaze and shrugged. She had to do what she had to do. That didn't mean she looked forward to facing the lion in his den.

Grabbing the printout, she stuffed it in the folder she'd prepared and hurried out of the cubicle to the director's office before he could leave. Or before she could change her mind. But the moment she stepped foot into his office, before she could so much as open her mouth, Mulvihill was already glowering at her.

"I thought I was clear about what I expected from you, Agent Fox."

"Just as I was clear about what I meant to do," Renata countered, placing the folder on his desk directly in front of him.

Mulvihill didn't even look at it. He shook his head and said, "So you're going for insubordination."

"I found a link between the City Sniper and Embry Lake."

In response, Mulvihill simply stared at her, his expression darkening. If the information surprised him, he was certainly hiding it well.

"Don't you even want to know—"

"I want you to stop digging where you don't belong!" Mulvihill shouted as he jumped to his feet.

Making Renata take a step back.

Why in the world was he suddenly so vehement? Because she'd brought up Embry Lake? Had he already known about the connection?

"If I don't belong working on a case important to S.A.F.E., as well as to the public I serve," Renata said, anger adding to her frustration, "then where do I belong?"

"Maybe out of this agency," Mulvihill said, suddenly sounding more exhausted than exasperated. "I'm satisfied this case is closed. What I'm not satisfied with is *you*. You're beginning to make me sorry I ever hired you. And if you pursue this issue further, or talk to one more media person, I promise I can fix that."

Her anger growing at the threat, Renata said, "Embry Lake, read the report," before turning her back on the director and walking out of his office, more determined than ever to learn the whole truth.

GABE HAD BEEN UNEASY ever since seeing Renata to her apartment door. If he'd expected her to call him, he would certainly have been disappointed. So he hadn't expected anything.

Instead, he'd gone home, showered, shaved and tried to get some sleep. But every time he closed his eyes, all he could see were flames…and Renata when she was about to pass out.

He had to see her to be sure she was okay.

After calling to make sure Renata was checked in at S.A.F.E., he waited across the street from the offices, with both the front exit and the alley in view. He intended to stay there and wait all night, if necessary. But of course it didn't take that long. He'd barely been in position for ten minutes before she exited via the loading dock. She cautiously looked around her, but somehow she didn't spot him.

Which made him realize she was distracted.

He watched her for a moment.

Tension oozed from her. She was angry. Undoubtedly his prediction that she wouldn't succeed in convincing Mulvihill of anything had come true. Of course not. Not when Mulvihill was hiding his own culpability.

How far would Mulvihill go to protect himself? Gabe wondered.

Murder?

Was he acting on his own, or did he have another pair of hands to do the dirty work?

How guilty was he?

Gabe was about to go to Renata when another man accosted her. She didn't look pleased. Tall and whipcord thin with a boyish face under spiked hair, the man was saying something that made her face redden.

Gabe picked up his pace and jogged across the street.

Renata turned away, but the man grabbed her by the arm and spun her around. Reacting quickly, she stomped his instep and threw her shoulder into him. He seemed about to reciprocate with a fist when a furious Gabe got to the man, spun him around and punched him in his boyish face.

"What the hell—"

The man flew for him and Gabe ducked too late. Knuckles made contact with his lip and the metallic taste of blood filled his mouth.

"Tag! Gabe!" Renata got between them. "Stop it!"

"Who is this jerk?" Tag asked her. He glared at Gabe. "I ought to arrest you for assaulting a federal officer!"

"I'm a friend of the lady, and she doesn't like to be touched. Respect that."

Now it was Renata touching *him*. She tugged at his arm to get him to move. "C'mon, Gabe. Tag, just drop it."

"You'll be sorry, Fox. You and your lover boy here."

Gabe whipped right around, asking, "Is that a threat?"

"Enough!" Renata said. "Tag, get lost. Gabe, let him go."

Tag glared at her, then stalked off.

"Where's the car?" Renata asked.

"A block over." He indicated the direction.

"Let's go."

Gabe simmered down and let her lead him away. "I assume that idiot is someone you work with?"

"Sort of. Tag Garvey is a sharpshooter, so he's part of the team."

"Sharpshooter."

"One of the men who shot Muti Hawass. He thinks I'm trying to make him and the others look bad." She glanced at him. "You're the one who looks bad." While they waited on the corner for the light to change, Renata dug in her shoulder bag and came up with a tissue. "Hold still a moment."

Wincing herself as she looked up at him, she tended to his lip, dabbing at the cut.

Calming down at her touch, Gabe suggested, "It would feel better if you kissed it."

He wanted nothing more than to take her in his arms. For a moment, their gazes locked and Gabe swore he saw a reflection of his own emotions.

Then she croaked, "Maybe later."

He grunted.

"I could have handled Tag myself," she informed him as the light changed and they crossed the street. "You should have let me."

"I didn't know who he was. He could have been the sniper. At least the person who's been after you. Considering what I know now, that seems totally credible."

"Tag? He's obnoxious, but he's Mr. Clean. He follows orders to the *T*, but he doesn't have an original thought of his own."

"Maybe he's taking orders from someone higher up," Gabe said, thinking of Mulvihill. Did this Garvey work for the director in an unofficial capacity?

Renata simply blinked at the suggestion, as if considering the possibility. Then she shook the thought away and asked, "What are you doing here, anyway?"

"Investigating."

"Investigating what?"

"My favorite subject—you. I wanted to see for myself if you got anywhere with your new report. I wish it had worked out for you."

She made a sound of disgust. "Can you read everyone this easily?"

"Some are easier than others."

But she was the easiest. Even though they'd only met a few days before, he felt as if he'd known her most of his life. An odd feeling.

When they arrived at the car, he opened the door for her and helped her in before getting behind the wheel and heading for Lake Shore Drive.

"Where are you taking me?"

"Time for some intellectual stimulation," he said.

"Clarify, please."

"A bookstore."

"Chuck LaRoe?"

"Chuck LaRoe."

Considering how the investigation hadn't been as thorough as it might have been if S.A.F.E. hadn't tagged Muti Hawass so fast, Gabe figured it wouldn't hurt to see what they could learn about Russell Ackerman's activities in Chicago once he'd donned the Chuck LaRoe identity. And that meant starting with his co-workers at Hawley's Bookstore, several miles north of the downtown area.

"You know, LaRoe's arrest makes more sense now," Gabe said, "in light of his being part of the Embry Lake Brigade. Their leader, Joshua Hague, took a stand against our military action in other countries, and Ackerman/LaRoe was arrested for participating in a war protest without a permit."

"And yet, we had it from a reliable source that Hague was conspiring with terrorists."

"If he really was," Gabe said. "I wouldn't be too sure about that." To his knowledge, the old man had been about protecting the homeland, not invasion. Sort of like the S.A.F.E. credo. "Sources have been known to be wrong, to lead good people to foolish deeds."

"Like killing Muti Hawass," she murmured. "He was thought to have associated with terrorists. Paul Broden, one of the agents I work with, thought that justified his being killed, whether or not he was guilty of being the City Sniper."

"Warped logic."

"But from what I gather, not uncommon at S.A.F.E.," Renata said, "and for all I know, maybe not at any law enforcement agency. Some people don't care how or why criminals are stopped, as long as someone stops them."

Is that what Mulvihill thought he was doing? Gabe wondered. Making people pay?

"Commit one crime and pay for another, but I don't see that as being justice," Renata said.

"That's because you're a straight arrow."

"What about you, Gabe? How straight an arrow are you in all this?"

"Hey, I already told you I'm your side. That I have a problem with someone being killed for something he didn't do."

Gabe wondered what was going on in Renata's mind. She knew where he stood on the issue, but she was still pressing him. He thought she trusted him, but maybe not. Or maybe she was simply getting nervous because of what had almost happened between them. Maybe she was looking for ethical differences, which, in her mind, was the easy way out.

She didn't have to look at all. No matter how he felt about her, no matter how much he felt for her, he wouldn't kid himself. Soon, she would know the whole truth about him, about why he was after Mulvihill, about Embry Lake…

And then she would turn her back on him, because what could he say in his own defense?

Chapter Thirteen

Hawley's Bookstore was located in a massive building that reminded Renata of a warehouse. The books were used—or pre-owned, as Hawley's advertised—mostly hardback, including lots of expensive coffee-table picture books.

When Renata identified herself and asked for the manager, she and Gabe were led back to Mickey Hamilton's office, a room with a desk, a couple of chairs, a single filing cabinet and stacks and stacks of books. Hamilton himself was youngish—maybe thirty—and dressed in black. His blond hair was spiked, both ears were pierced and he wore funky little dark-framed glasses.

"Agent Fox," Hamilton said after glancing at her identification and indicating they should sit. "What can I do for you?"

Thankful he didn't ask to see Gabe's ID, she said, "We're continuing the investigation into Chuck LaRoe's murder."

"I thought you had the guy. That terrorist."

"Maybe. But we want to look deeper."

"Aha, you mean you're looking for a motive," the manager said knowingly.

Probably a mystery reader, Renata thought. "Right, we're trying to figure out motive."

Hamilton spread his hands and looked from her to Gabe. "I'm afraid I've told you people everything I know about Chuck. Which isn't much."

"You never know what could have gotten overlooked," Gabe said.

Willing him to leave the questioning to her, Renata gave Gabe an annoyed look, then felt guilty. He'd put himself on the line for her, had risked his life saving hers. Official or not, he was as much a part of this investigation as she was. Gabe caught her gaze and the way he looked at her with such intensity made her stomach tumble even as she turned her attention back to the manager.

"Why don't you start at the beginning," she suggested, "and describe the circumstances around your hiring Chuck LaRoe."

"I placed a sign for help in the window, he came in and filled in the application. I hired him. Simple."

"What about references?"

"As I told you people before, I was desperate for help at the time, so I hired him. I meant to check out the references, but I never did."

"Why not?"

"He was good at what he did. Customers liked him. Hell, I liked him."

"The application—do you still have it?"

"I already gave it to you people."

Renata tried not to be offended by his using *you people* as if he were lumping her in his mind with every other officer of the law. Probably he did.

"You gave it to whom?" she asked. "Chicago police or S.A.F.E.?"

"I don't remember now."

Then he must have given it to someone from the CPD. She'd been through LaRoe's file more than once and the application hadn't been in there or she would have remembered seeing it.

"Do you remember any of the names of those references?"

"You gotta be kidding. That was months ago."

"What about friends?" Gabe asked.

Renata chanced a glance his way and was grateful Gabe's attention was on the manager rather than on her. Bad enough she got distracted by his simply being there.

"I know nothing about Chuck's life away from the bookstore," Hamilton was saying. "He was a guy who liked his privacy."

Renata asked, "What about *in* the bookstore? Was he friendly with anyone in particular?" If so, perhaps that person might have a better handle on the man.

"Not that I ever noticed," the manager said. "Chuck usually kept to himself. He had a good rapport with the customers, but he really didn't go out of his way to be friendly with the staff."

"Didn't you find that unusual?"

"Writers are often solitary people who live in their

heads," Hamilton said, as if he knew this from personal experience.

"Writers?" Renata echoed. "You're saying Chuck LaRoe was writing something?"

"Well, yeah. A book. A couple of us got into this discussion of how difficult it was to come up with a really great idea. And Chuck overheard us and said reality is sometimes stranger than fiction. And more lucrative. So I asked him if he was writing a book based on something that really happened. He admitted as much."

"What kind of a book?" Gabe asked.

"It had to do with a murder, so either a mystery or thriller," Hamilton said.

Or true crime, Renata thought, though she didn't say it.

The manager went on. "Chuck was real funny about it all, like as soon as it came out of his mouth he regretted saying anything. Wouldn't give me any details. But he said it was something that was going to make him a lot of money, get him out of the bookstore biz. Though why he'd want to do that, I don't know."

"So that was the end of the conversation?" she asked. "Nothing about the crime itself?"

"Nope. That was it, other than my saying he had to get whatever his manuscript was published first. And then Chuck said not necessarily. Now that threw me. I figured he was just whacked."

Unless Ackerman/LaRoe really had knowledge that was worth selling, Renata thought. She asked the manager a few more questions, but she could get nothing more promising out of him, so they left.

But Renata knew they'd stumbled onto at least part of truth.

Now the challenge was to find the rest of it and figure out how to fit the pieces together so that it all made sense.

LANDING AT CLUB UNDERCOVER shortly after opening, Renata was glad to have a quick meal and some time to settle down and renew her brain a bit. Time to catch her breath was becoming nonexistent in her world.

All too soon she and Gabe were meeting with the rest of Team Undercover in the employee lounge, where they quickly shared the various bits of information they'd dug up on Chuck LaRoe and his alter ego. Their big finish was their near disastrous venture into Michigan. Renata was thankful Gabe gave an edited version of the fire, leaving out what they'd been doing when she'd smelled smoke.

Just thinking about what had been happening between them made her twist in her chair and cross her legs.

Feeling watched, she turned to meet Cass's knowing gaze. Renata's cheeks burned as she turned her attention back to Gideon.

"You two certainly have had your share of excitement," the club owner was saying. "You could have been killed."

"But we weren't, which is the important part," Renata said, trying not to think too closely on how many times her life had been in jeopardy in the past week.

"You learned more than we did," Cass said. "We tried following the Michigan connection for the various people on your list and only came up with one."

"Chuck LaRoe, right?" Renata asked.

"Not even close," Gideon said. "Try Congressman Carl Cooper."

She tensed, asking, "What kind of connection?"

"You'll appreciate this one in light of everything you just told us about Embry Lake. He was there."

"At Embry Lake?" Gabe asked. "When?"

"At the standoff. He was there to make a firsthand report to the committee on S.A.F.E. activities."

Stunned, Renata said, "How in the world…you didn't find that in the media."

"As a matter of fact, I didn't," Gideon said. "Cass had some strong feelings about the congressman being connected to a tragedy in Michigan, and when we couldn't bring up anything in our Internet research, I pulled some strings with a government contact who confirmed that information."

Government contact. Renata wanted to ask Gideon who the heck he really was, but she knew he would be no more open about his past and motivations than Gabe. As had been happening to her with increasing frequency lately, she was feeling out of her depth.

"The Embry Lake massacre seems to be the key to everything," Gabe mused. "We can tie Maè Chin to Cooper. Same with Heidi Bourne. That makes three of the five victims."

Not even wanting to think about the political ramifications if she brought this information to light, Renata said, "But how do Maurice Washington and Gary Hudson fit in? A drug dealer and a lawyer…"

"No Michigan connections that we could find," Gideon said. "Sorry."

"There's nothing to be sorry about." Renata took a big breath. "Embry Lake happened before I became a S.A.F.E. agent, but I don't ever remember reading or hearing about Congressman Cooper being there. I wonder why."

"He simply could have been trying to lay low after what happened," Blade said. "I know something about raids going wrong and the cover-ups that follow."

"I hope you're right," Renata said. "I would hate to think the congressman who sponsored S.A.F.E. in the first place is guilty of murder."

The things he already had been accused of were more than enough to discredit him, Renata thought. Or at least they would have been if the prosecution's chief witness against him hadn't been murdered.

"Let's go back to LaRoe/Ackerman," Gabe said. "The bookstore manager said he was writing a book about something real that happened."

Having come to the same conclusion, Renata said, "Embry Lake. If he had something new to say, of course." One book had already been published and another was on the way.

"He boasted about the money it would make… whether or not it got published," Gabe said.

"Blackmail." Cass seemed a little distant, as if she were trying to picture something in her mind. "Did anyone ever find a manuscript?"

"Not to my knowledge," Renata said.

"So he was writing a book he thought someone would pay him to destroy." Gabe's expression tightened. "What if that someone had him murdered, then destroyed the evidence. Someone tore his place apart; that could be why."

Renata mused, "But why? What about Embry Lake made *his* firsthand account so valuable?"

"Apparently he saw something at Embry Lake that the murderer didn't want revealed."

"But that could be only one thing I can think of," Renata said. Pulse racing, she added, "The identity of the person who fired the first shot and started the massacre!"

"Bingo."

"Which means the person who wanted to see Ackerman/LaRoe dead could be one of his own—someone who also survived Embry Lake," Gideon said.

"Maybe even Hank Oeland, and maybe not over the widow." Renata prayed Oeland was the one, because she didn't want to consider the alternative.

She didn't want to look too closely at the people she worked with at S.A.F.E.

SO, HAD THEY nailed it or what? Gabe wondered, excitement pulsing through him. Soon, justice would be done and Danny could rest a little easier.

Rather, *he* could.

"What if it wasn't Oeland who fired the first shot?" he asked Renata.

"What are you suggesting?"

"No one ever discovered how the massacre started. That smells of a cover-up to me. Congressman Cooper was there, but not as far as the media was concerned. Elliott Mulvihill has to be involved."

Gabe watched the color drain from Renata's face and felt a moment of regret. She wanted so badly to believe in the system, and, he figured, to believe in Mulvihill, no matter how badly her boss had been treating her.

"Are you saying you think Director Mulvihill took the first shot himself?"

"Why not?" Gabe asked. "He certainly would have been armed. No particular bullet was identified as being the first shot. What if Mulvihill fired and Ackerman saw him do it? Then Ackerman sees Mulvihill being promoted and knows he could have a pretty sweet deal since Mulvihill wouldn't want that to be common knowledge."

"So you think he blackmailed Mulvihill…and Mulvihill killed him?" Renata said.

"Why not?"

Renata stared at him, her expression odd, and Gabe feared she was starting to figure things out.

But rather than press him, she turned to Blade and asked, "Did you get that list of sharpshooters in the area?"

"Right here. It's pretty comprehensive."

Blade handed her the list and she quickly scanned

it. When she looked up, her expression showed her relief. "Mulvihill's name isn't on this list." She folded the list and put it in her shoulder bag.

"It wouldn't take a sharpshooter simply to fire a gun and start a war between a government agency and a militia," Gabe argued. "The first round could have been from a handgun as easily as a rifle with a scope."

"But the City Sniper used a rifle—"

"We've already considered the sniper could have been hired by someone," Gabe said. "Mulvihill could have done that. Or maybe he directed someone under his command to do his dirty work."

Renata shook her head. "But what about the others? Five people were murdered!"

"Three of whom we can link to Congressman Cooper, who was at Embry Lake," he reminded her. "And Mulvihill got promoted. Cooper's recommendation?"

Renata didn't argue, though he saw her mind wasn't made up. Not that Gabe expected it to be, not without proof.

Once they got it—once he could prove his quest was justified—would she understand and forgive him for deceiving her about his motivation?

"YOU'RE AWFULLY QUIET," Gabe said as they entered his apartment.

Renata hadn't argued about going home with him. Her only alternative was a hotel room and she didn't want to be alone. Not tonight, certainly.

"I'm trying to take it all in," she admitted.

Slipping out of her jacket, she let Gabe take it from her. She didn't want to believe the conclusions she was coming to, but how could she not? Renata thought, removing her holster and hanging her weapon from the back of a chair.

"The night I met you—" Renata began "—just as I was waiting for the elevator...I saw Director Mulvihill come out of his office with Congressman Cooper. I didn't really draw any conclusions at the time, since Cooper has that connection with S.A.F.E. Maybe I should have. The way the congressman stared at me..."

A chill ran down her spine as she remembered his glare and thinking he knew who she was.

Had that been the start of it all? Mulvihill and Cooper planning her demise?

Having hung up their jackets, Gabe moved to her and pulled her into his arms. "It's almost over," he murmured into her hair. "Everything's going to be all right."

His arms around her felt so good; she wanted to relax. "You can't be sure of that."

"I'm as sure as anyone can be of anything."

"Why?"

"Because I believe in you." He drew back enough that he could see into her eyes. "I believe in us. Together, we'll find proof—"

"You believe in us?" she echoed, her heart thumping against her ribs.

"We make an unstoppable team."

"Oh."

And here she thought he was getting to something more private. It certainly felt as if it should be, her being in his arms and all, with his body pressed against hers, hips to hips, breasts to chest. It was a good feeling. A right feeling. A feeling she wanted to grab on to.

"I thought maybe you meant something more personal," she said.

Gabe's low, sexy voice vibrated through her when he asked, "Do you want it to be more personal?"

"I kind of thought it already was. I mean, after last night…"

She let her words trail off because she was afraid to voice her true thoughts.

"Last night was pretty scary," Gabe said.

"I mean before the fire."

"So do I. Renata, I've never known anyone quite like you."

The breath quivered in her throat. Or maybe it was her pulse fluttering. She'd never felt like this before with any other man. Not that she hadn't had her share of attraction and satisfaction. She just hadn't wanted to make any of the men before permanent fixtures in her life. But Gabe was different. She'd known him for less than a week and couldn't imagine life without him.

Was this what love was like? she wondered, too afraid to put the question into words.

Instead, she asked with her eyes. From his expression, Gabe understood perfectly.

"Renata…" he breathed, catching her lips with his.

She snaked her arms around his neck and snaked her body along his. Wanting more than a kiss, more than a tease, she did her best to seduce him.

Not that it took much effort.

Gabe was ready for her. He anticipated her every move. And while they kissed and touched and rubbed against each other, he danced her around the room to turn off the lights, all but a night-light in the kitchen area. For a moment, she thought he was going to get that one, too, but it must have seemed too far away, too much trouble, for he stopped her at the sofa bed and leaned her against the back.

"What are you doing?" she asked breathlessly as he began sliding her narrow skirt upwards.

His features were taut, intense. "Strip-searching you. Any objections?"

"Not yet," she said with an excited laugh.

His hands slid along her stockings and stopped when they got to the bare flesh of her thighs. "No panty hose," he murmured. "Did you wear these for me?"

"Mmm."

"Not talking, huh?" he murmured softly. "Then I'll have to keep up the search, maybe torture you a little."

True to his promise, he peeled back her silk panties to one side, his fingers spreading her damp flesh and doing unspeakably exciting things to her. She unbuttoned her blouse and arched her back and magically his mouth found her breasts, his tongue catching one nipple, then the other, beneath the lace edging of her bra.

She wanted to touch and taste him, too, but suddenly it was all she could do to balance herself against the back of the sofa bed. She didn't dare let go lest she tumble backward, taking him with her headfirst into the cushions. So for once in her life, at least, she gave up control.

And Gabe was making the most of every second. He nuzzled her breasts, then made his way down her stomach, his beard stubble raising her flesh where they met. She was coiled tight inside. She needed release. Yet she wouldn't give up one second of the pleasure he gave her.

He nipped the soft flesh of her belly, then explored lower, nipping at her thighs, nuzzling the swollen wet flesh between them.

"Ahh…"

Renata almost came right then, right at the first touch of his tongue, but she held on, let him draw out the pleasure for as long as he would. But she was only human, and within seconds found herself giving over to the pleasure, hips rocking, breasts heaving, head tossing.

Just as she began to light from the inside out, he stopped. But before she could protest, he was stretched up over her, prodding her for entrance. She opened for him and he pushed in all the way. A few seconds of in-depth contact and sensual friction and sensation detonated inside her, and she wrapped her legs around his thighs to keep him there, to keep the stunning sensations coming.

He tried to kiss her, but she wanted to tantalize him now, finding the soft flesh between his neck and shoulder, first sucking, then biting down. As her teeth nicked his flesh, he stiffened and cried out and shuddered against her. She clung tight and shuddered again, too.

They stayed like that for what seemed like forever—wrapped in each other's arms, balanced on the back of the sofa bed.

Then passion faded and Renata realized they were both mostly still dressed and she wondered what she was doing tangled so intimately with a man she really didn't know.

But a voice inside her protested that, even though she didn't know all the details of his life, didn't know exactly why he was with her, she did know Gabe in the most basic way. She knew he was a good man. She knew he had saved her life. She knew he had put his own in jeopardy for her. What more did she need? What had just happened between them had been inevitable.

Danger might have pushed them together, but deeper emotions had taken over.

As Gabe pulled away to give her a soft, lingering kiss, Renata admitted to herself what she'd been afraid to examine too closely.

She didn't just care for the man…she was in love with him.

Chapter Fourteen

Light coming through the window left Renata wide awake, despite the fact that she'd had barely three hours of sleep—she and Gabe had spent the better part of the night and the early morning hours exploring each other. He lay next to her now, snoring softly, his dark hair tousled against the pillow. Her heart skipped a beat just looking at him. She loved his face, wanted to rub her cheek against his dark beard stubble. More, wanted to touch other parts of him intimately.

But as much as she wanted all that, she figured she wanted to be able to walk, as well—not to mention needing to concentrate on the case. More intimacy could wait. The killer couldn't.

Seeing that it was almost nine, she slid out of bed, put on a pot of coffee and then slipped into the bathroom, where she took a long, relaxing shower before wrapping herself in the robe Gabe had loaned her.

Part of her anticipated Gabe being awake and waiting for her when she came out of the bathroom, but to her disappointment, he was still asleep. So she poured herself a cup of that coffee. Noise from behind her told her that Gabe was stirring.

"Coffee?" she asked softly, just in case he wasn't really awake.

He grunted an answer in return.

As she poured, Gabe rolled out of bed and stalked toward her, naked as a jaybird.

Pulse fluttering, she stared into his eyes and stuck the mug between them.

"What, no morning kiss?" he asked.

"Shower first."

And put on some clothes, she thought, already imagining the things they would do if he didn't.

"You really aren't a morning person, are you?" he asked, lips quirking as he took the mug from her.

The grin nearly did her in.

"Shower," she groused, fighting her primal urges. "We have work to do."

Lives to save. Theirs.

"What, no soft words for the man you made love to all night?"

Warmth washed through her at the reminder. "I'm trying to be strong."

Gabe laughed, swiped her with a kiss anyway before heading for the bathroom, saying, "You'd better be dressed before I get out of the shower."

"Or what?"

"Stay in that robe and see," he threatened.

Ridiculously happy, Renata was tempted. She would like nothing better than to stay in bed with

Gabe all day, make mad, passionate love and forget everything else. Forget that her career was teetering, that someone was trying to kill her, that her mother would be a wreck no matter the outcome, because the truth about everything that had happened would come out in the end.

But she couldn't forget.

So as she heard the shower start in the bathroom, she fully dressed except for her holster and jacket. Unable to relax, she thought about all that was riding on their digging out the rest of the truth about the City Sniper. Needing something to keep her occupied, she decided to use Gabe's computer, which he'd left on. Sitting down before it, she meant to work the Internet and search for information on Congressman Cooper.

And on Director Mulvihill, she thought, switching on the monitor.

Mulvihill...

Seeing his name already on Gabe's computer screen, she froze. Gabe had a folder named Mulvihill displayed on his desktop?

Pulse ticking, she clicked open the folder only to find file after file filled with articles about Embry Lake. Articles he'd collected before they'd even made the Michigan connection.

Rather, before *she* had.

"What the hell!" she said aloud.

"Something wrong?"

She whipped around to see Gabe standing in the bathroom doorway, clad only in a towel anchored around his hips. His body still damp, he was rubbing at his wet hair with a hand towel. Seeing him like this, she should be turned on, Renata thought. But not a fiber of her being stirred; she was too afraid of what she had found.

His gaze flicked behind her at the monitor, and from the way his smile faded, she knew he knew.

Her stomach knotted. She didn't want to make assumptions. She didn't want to say the wrong thing. So she waited for him to tell her.

"What's the problem?" he asked lightly.

As if he didn't know...

"You tell me."

"Renata—"

"No, I mean it. Tell me and tell me now." When he stood there, staring at her, she added, "The truth, Gabe. Don't you think it's time you told me the truth about your interest in the City Sniper case?"

He heaved a sigh and merely said, "It's Mulvihill," as if that's all she needed to hear.

"I can see that," she said, indicating the screen. "But what about him?"

"He's the reason I sought you out," Gabe admitted. "I figured it was time someone made him pay for the things he'd done."

"What things?"

She stared at him, willed him to talk, but now he kept tight-lipped. He didn't have to say it, though, for her to know that he'd used her. He'd wanted her to find dirt on her boss for him. But still he wouldn't tell her why. Furious with him, feeling betrayed, Renata grabbed her shoulder holster, fastened it and covered it with her jacket.

She met Gabe's gaze one last time, hoping he would tell her the whole truth at last, that he would be able to explain away what he'd done. That he would tell her why he'd lied about his brother simply because Danny had been in the wrong place at the wrong time.

But he said nothing. He'd shut down. He obviously wasn't going to try to save himself.

Or them.

But as she got to the door, he did say, "Renata, wait."

She waited, her hand on the doorknob, though she refused to turn around and look at him.

"Last night…last night was real."

She closed her eyes. It had been real for her, at least. But she hadn't known everything. If she had, last night would never have happened.

Without so much as a backward glance, she left, slamming the door behind her.

Who the hell *was* Gabe?

And how many times had she asked herself that question?

Now was the time to find out.

She hoofed it over to a main street where she was lucky enough to flag down a taxi. They went north, straight to Broadway Electronics. The store wasn't open, of course. It was Sunday; it wouldn't be open until noon. That gave her more than an hour to kill before she could get information about Gabe himself.

Spotting a family restaurant across the street, she decided to get something to eat. Not that she was hungry. It was too early.

Thinking about how Gabe had used her, Renata thought she might never be hungry again.

Commandeering a booth at the window, she kept watch while forcing herself to eat half a breakfast. Her throat was tight and that's all she could get down as she tried to block herself from thinking about her personal relationship with Gabe.

Pulling out her cell phone, she tried distracting herself from her teeming emotions by picking up her messages. Of course, even though she'd stopped by to let her mom know she would be gone, the worrywart had called three times, twice yesterday and once this morning.

She took a deep breath and got connected.

"Renata, thank goodness you're all right," her mom said anxiously.

"Of course I'm all right."

"What's wrong with your voice?"

"Sinuses. Something in Michigan didn't agree with me."

She didn't add that massive amounts of smoke wouldn't agree with anyone. Her biggest hope was that her mom never had to hear about any of the terrible things that had happened to her on this case.

"Have you seen a doctor?"

"Actually, I have. I'll be as good as new in a day or two." Assuming she was still alive.

"So did you have a good time?"

Renata swallowed hard and sought a truth she could tell her mother. "It wasn't boring."

"That Gabe fellow seems pretty nice."

"Yes, he does seem that way."

"You sound odd, honey. Is something wrong?"

"You know how it is when you like someone and you're afraid it isn't going to work out."

"You don't think he cares for you?"

"I don't know, Mom. I thought so…but…we'll see."

She was saved from further interrogation when she spotted Ned Coulter getting out of his car.

"Mom, I have to go. Business. Talk to you later."

And before the woman could get in another word, Renata powered down her cell, grabbed the bill and ran to the register, where she left enough money to include a huge tip.

Waiting until there was a break in traffic, Renata ran across Broadway, catching up to Coulter just as he opened the front door of his business. An instant of concern passed through his features before he recovered.

"Agent Fox," he said, looking behind her. "Nice to see you again."

"Gabe's not with me this time. Let's go inside."

Coulter led the way and got the lights. "What can I do for you? I told you I didn't know anything about Ackerman other than his name."

"What about Gabe?" she asked.

"What do you mean?"

"What's *his* name?"

Silence ticked between them. She practically could see Coulter's mind racing.

"Don't lie to me, Coulter, or I'll shut you down," Renata threatened.

"You said you would forget—"

"No," she interrupted. "Gabe said that."

"But you didn't contradict him. I expect you to keep to the promise."

"And I expect you to give me a name." If she was going to check Gabe out, she needed to know who he really was. "Don't screw with me, Coulter. I'm serious about this."

"If I tell you, you'll leave me alone?"

"If you give me the truth, then yes, I promise."

"And you won't tell Gabe I gave you the name?"

"It doesn't matter. He'll know. So give, Coulter."

The man tightened his jaw, then said, "All right. Griffith. Gabriel Griffith."

"You're sure that's his *real* name?"

"I couldn't swear on it. But that's the name he was using when he came to me."

"If you're lying, I'll be back," she threatened, making for the door.

Griffith...

Now why did that sound so familiar?

She thought about it as she ascended the stairs to the train platform. Griffith. Gabriel Griffith.

But no matter how many times she rolled it over in her mind, she simply couldn't place it.

GABE SPENT THE MORNING beating himself up. Why hadn't he told Renata everything?

Now she would never trust him.

Even as he thought it, he knew that if he had told her before, she would have been gone. She hadn't wanted his help in the first place. Now she must be thinking she'd been a fool to let him force his way into her investigation.

And especially into her life.

This had been a "lose-lose" situation for him when it came to Renata. He only hoped learning that he was still keeping information from her wouldn't deter her from finishing her investigation.

Wanting to go after her, he held himself back. She would be in no mood to talk so soon. She needed some time to cool down, time to put things into perspective, so she would listen to reason. Even if she never wanted to see him again personally, surely he could persuade her to let him help finish what they'd started.

But to do that, he would have to tell her everything. Maybe she would even understand.

Trying to distract himself from thoughts of Renata while getting further information that would help them resolve the case, he logged onto the computer and fed "Congressman Carl Cooper" into a search engine. Within seconds, thousands of links appeared. He began clicking on them one at a time, running searches through the articles about Embry Lake. About Mulvihill, too. But his efforts were futile.

After several hours of frustration, he'd had enough.

Not knowing what to do with himself, he headed over to the club. At least there, he had people who trusted him.

Why couldn't Renata? he wondered.

She should know him well enough by now.

So he'd left out a little detail. Well, maybe a big detail. That didn't change who he was.

How could she not see that?

His mood agitated, Gabe entered the club and headed for the kitchen, where he got one of the cooks to make him a burger. He was at the bar eating when Cass walked in.

The moment she spotted him, she headed his way. But when she got within several feet of him, she stopped and frowned. Halfway through the burger, Gabe set it down and stared back at her. The skin along his spine began to crawl.

Swallowing, he said, "Hey, Cass, what's up?"

"That's my question for you. What *is* up? And where's Renata?"

Realizing she was reading him, he tried to relax. "I don't know. Off somewhere investigating, I assume." He tore another bite of his burger.

"And you let her go alone?"

Mouth full, he said, "I'm not her keeper."

"I thought you cared about her."

The food in Gabe's mouth went dry. He chased it down with a long swallow of water, then said, "Okay, Cass, give. What did you see?"

"I shouldn't have to tell you. You know she's not safe."

"Sorry. Not specific enough. Did you see something or not?"

"Just a flash…"

"Of what?"

"Fear."

Gabe cursed under his breath, then said, "Not enough. Fear of what? Where is she?"

Gray eyes wide, Cass shook her head. "I don't know, Gabe. Honestly."

"On the street? In an alley?"

"Inside."

"Her apartment?"

Cass shook her head. "But someplace familiar."

That was the problem with Cass's psychic visions—they were never clear. But this one was clear enough for Gabe to make an educated guess.

He gave Cass a quick squeeze and hurried out of Club Undercover, wondering how the heck he was going to get into the S.A.F.E. building.

RENATA WAS THANKFUL it was late Sunday afternoon, which meant a limited number of people would be around the S.A.F.E. offices. She could get at the records she needed with no Mulvihill to stop her.

The first thing she did was to search S.A.F.E. records for "Gabriel Griffith." When she couldn't find anything to implicate Gabe, relief inched through her bit by bit.

At least he didn't seem to be on someone's Most Wanted list. At least not under that name.

Renata took a deep breath. She hadn't really expected to find anything against Gabe, yet she'd had to check. She couldn't trust her own judgment.

Or could she?

Gabe had asked her to trust him and, in fact, she had. She hadn't been sorry—not until that morning.

And when he'd pulled her out of the burning motel room, she'd been quite grateful.

Why couldn't Gabe have been honest with her that morning, if not before?

Because he didn't trust her.

She sat back and thought about it. Gabe didn't trust *her*. That had to be it.

Another why.

Wanting to make the most of her time, lest the wrong person find her and force her to leave, she focused her attention on the case itself.

On Congressman Carl Cooper.

"Let's see what we have on you, Congressman."

But the only connection she found was to his position on the committee that approved and funded S.A.F.E. Nothing about Embry Lake.

She inputted "Embry Lake" on their closed computer system but still could get nothing on Cooper. But when she scanned the report and got to the list of the victims and saw the name above leader Joshua Hague's, she was shocked.

Hardly able to make a sound, she whispered the name, "Daniel Griffith."

That's why the name Griffith had been so familiar. She'd read it over and over again for months.

Daniel Griffith…*Danny*…this had to be Gabe's brother Danny.

Renata felt as if the breath had been knocked out of her.

It all made sense now. Gabe had told her his brother Danny had been an innocent killed because he'd been in the wrong place at the wrong time. No wonder Gabe blamed Mulvihill—he'd been in charge of the operation gone wrong.

But if Daniel Griffith was an innocent, why had he been at the Embry Lake compound in the first place?

Whatever the reason, her heart went out to Gabe.

He hadn't trusted her because she was a government agent working for the very agency responsible for his brother's death. No doubt he thought if he told her everything, she wouldn't have believed him, that she would have discounted his zeal immediately as being that of a survivor of one of the victims and thereby unreliable.

Now Renata thought she understood.

Still, there was something missing…

There was only one thing to do. She had to face Gabe and get him to fill in the blanks. But not now. Now she had to take advantage of being in the S.A.F.E. offices, on the S.A.F.E. computer, perhaps for the last time. This might be her only opportunity to unearth the truth. Once Mulvihill got wind of her activities, she would probably be fired, barred from the premises for good.

So Renata continued to go through the Embry Lake records with a fine-tooth comb. She was determined to stay put for hours, if necessary, going over details until her mind couldn't absorb another fact.

But it was only minutes before she received another surprise. Agent Paul Broden had been at Embry Lake under Mulvihill's command. What she hadn't known was that Broden had passed on the information from an unidentified informant about the supposed terrorists working with the Embry Lake Brigade.

What did this mean? she wondered. Broden had tried to make her back down in the City Sniper investigation, had said they all made mistakes. Was that his mistake? Passing on bad information?

She began a list of every name associated with Embry Lake—militia and other townspeople on one side, S.A.F.E. and other authority figures in the other column. One of these people had started a war that ended with nine dead. Could one of their compatriots—Hank Oeland?—have condemned them? Or had it been one of the "good guys?"

Tag Garvey was on that list. Tag Garvey had been giving her a hell of a time. Could he have fired the first shot? she wondered, bringing up his records. He was capable of being the City Sniper. But to what purpose? Ackerman/LaRoe had information someone would pay for—the name of the person who'd fired the first shot? Tag? Had Tag killed him to shut him up? By why the others?

She decided to scan his employment file, starting with his application.

Within minutes, a new truth left her breathless. Every employee needed good recommendations, and Tag had gotten one that would be sure to get him the job: Congressman Carl Cooper himself.

Her mind whirled.

Cooper had connections to three of the victims, to Mulvihill at Embry Lake, now to one of the sharpshooters. Did he have connections to all of the victims? Had he gotten Tag to do his dirty work for him?

If not Tag, who else could it be?

Remembering the list of sharpshooters Blade had given her, Renata rummaged through her shoulder bag until she found it. Wanting to see if there were any other possible shooters, she held it up next to the list she'd compiled of people who'd been at Embry Lake.

Another match…one she hadn't noticed when she'd quickly taken that glance at Club Undercover. She picked up a pen and circled the name in red.

Could it really be…?

Stunned, Renata mentally examined everything that had happened since she'd blown the whistle on what she'd considered to be sloppy investigative work…everything that had been said to her… everything that she and Gabe had learned over the past week…

What if it had been more than sloppy investigative work? What if it had been a cover-up that reached farther than she could have imagined?

She powered down the computer and gathered lists and printouts and shoved them into her shoulder bag.

She had to get to Gabe and show him this. She had to tell him she trusted him to see her through this.

She *did* trust Gabe.

No matter how troubled she had been by his secrecy, she had trusted him all along. If she hadn't, how could she have fallen in love with him? Maybe if she told him that, he would trust her, as well.

Anxious to see Gabe, Renata rose to leave and stopped short when she nearly ran into the man blocking her cubicle exit. Her pulse did a loop-the-loop and she was left speechless. She wondered how quickly she could get to her weapon.

"Going somewhere?" asked the man responsible for the Embry Lake massacre and the City Sniper shootings.

Now he'd come for her in person.

Chapter Fifteen

"Let this work," Gabe muttered as he made his way into the S.A.F.E. building via the loading dock.

It was one of the slipperiest plans he'd ever conjured, but he was counting on the late hour, on the tiredness and inattention of whoever was working on a Sunday night and on that person's knowledge of Renata's using the back route since her story broke in the media the week before.

"Can I help you?" asked the security guard behind the glass window the moment he stepped inside.

Noting he'd pulled the young man from his computer game, Gabe flashed the ID that Ned Coulter had just made for him. "I'm meeting Agent Renata Fox," he said. "She hasn't left yet, has she?"

"She hasn't been through here to leave yet," the guard said. "But I can call her for you."

"Please."

Not that Gabe knew what her reaction would be if she actually answered the phone. The guard was under the mistaken impression—via the ID, of course—that he was FBI Agent Gabriel Martin.

But the guard never got a chance to ask her. He shook his head and hung up when she didn't answer. And Gabe's chest tightened. What if she was in trouble just as Cass had predicted?

"Why don't I take a stroll upstairs and find her myself?" he suggested far more casually than he was feeling.

"Sign in, then," the clerk said, turning back to his video game.

And so Gabe did.

The clerk buzzed him through, and Gabe hesitated, saying, "Ninth floor, right?"

"Eleventh."

He snapped his fingers as if he'd just remembered and gave the clerk an embarrassed smile. Then he swept into the hallway and headed straight for the freight elevator, where he punched the up button. This was one of those old renovated buildings in the south Loop, the *old* punctuated by the length of time it took the elevator to descend.

When he'd gone to see Ned Coulter for the new ID, the man had been a case of nerves and had tried to tell him that he had to leave for an important appointment. Knowing something was wrong, Gabe hadn't accepted the brush off. He'd made the man talk. And now he knew that Renata knew he wasn't really Gabriel Connor.

What she didn't know was that he wasn't Gabriel Griffith, either.

The elevator arrived just as he was contemplating using the stairs. He had a sick feeling. Why had he ever let Renata's anger push him away, even for a few hours?

Punching 11—one floor from the top—he only hoped he wouldn't be too late.

If anything happened to her, he would be to blame.

HE HAD HER AT LAST, the killer thought. She knew she was done for—he could smell the fear on her.

"Don't make any sudden moves," he said, slipping his hand out of his pocket to show her his gun. "Put down the shoulder bag."

She did as commanded. "I don't understand—"

"Of course you do. You're bright. Too bright. Too bad for you. Up with the hands."

She did as he said while straining for a look over his shoulder. No one was left on this floor. Even if someone was around, it wouldn't be anyone who would lift a finger to help her. He had it all worked out in his mind. And if something went wrong—if someone saw—he could claim she'd gone off on him, and he'd simply been trying to restrain her.

He patted her down to make certain she wasn't wearing a shoulder holster. Good. No doubt the gun was in the leather bag now decorating her desk.

"You can't possibly think you can get away with killing me," she said.

"Why not? I've gotten away with much more than that. I've killed tougher opponents than you. But you, I think I'm going to enjoy most."

"You're sick."

"This country is sick. I'm one of the sane ones, cleaning up the messes."

"Is that how you see what you've done?"

"You're not going to stall me, not here, not where someone could walk in on us." He waved the Glock, indicating she should move out of her cubicle. "Let's go someplace more private so we can *talk*."

If she bought that, she really was a fool.

GABE GOT OFF on the eleventh floor and found his way through to the main hall. Now all he had to do was find Renata.

Entering a large office filled with work cubicles, he started checking them. He poked his head inside each one as he passed it, but no sign of her.

Empty...empty...empty...

Then an agent looked up from his computer. "Can I help you?"

"Wrong cubicle," Gabe muttered, going on, hoping the guy wouldn't follow him and demand to know his business.

Hearing what sounded like footsteps and a low voice through a door opening, he headed that way, which meant going through the next room, a big one basically like the first. Gabe scanned this room fast, and halfway through, nearly passed Renata's cubicle.

But at the last minute, he caught sight of the leather shoulder bag that had been discarded on the desk. Some papers poked from the open mouth.

Normally, he wouldn't go through a woman's

purse, but this was an exception. When he picked it up, the weight of the thing nearly threw him until he remembered she sometimes used a holster specially built into the bottom of the bag. Unzipping it, he withdrew her Glock and pocketed the handgun.

And heard another noise…the sound of a heavy door opening and clicking closed.

Taking a quick look at the papers, his eye caught the red circle around one name on the list Blade had given her.

The City Sniper…

MORE CALMLY than she was feeling, Renata said, "You were the one who fired the first shot at Embry Lake, weren't you?"

He'd taken her into a stairwell and was pushing her upward. She assumed he meant to kill her somewhere on the stairs and leave her body to be found by the cleaning staff at some indeterminate date in the future.

"You're even smarter than I gave you credit for," he admitted, poking her in the back with the gun to keep her going. "Tell me the rest."

"Russell Ackerman saw you do it," she said with certainty. "He wasn't the one who died in the fire. He moved to Chicago, created a new identity for himself and dabbled with the idea of writing a book about the massacre. But first, Ackerman tried to blackmail you."

He whistled, the sound indicating surprise. "Ackerman laid low for a while, but he knew where to find me. He started haunting me, threatening me, saying that his book would reveal everything he knew, starting with his seeing me taking that first shot. I knew I had to get rid of him and his work."

"So you tore up his place, trying to find the manuscript. Was there one?" she asked.

"What would pass for one. He hid it in a zipped plastic bag in the toilet tank."

Renata stopped when the stairs ended at a metal door.

"You would have been a valuable asset to S.A.F.E.," he said, so close behind her she could feel the breath on her hair. "It's a shame you have to die."

He reached around her with his free hand to open the door, then nudged her into the night with the barrel of the gun pressing against her spine. It took her eyes a moment to adjust, but the moon was nearly full and pipes and air-conditioning units on the flat roof stood out in blue-rimmed clarity.

They were thirteen stories up. Unlucky thirteen. How appropriate, she thought, as he kept nudging her closer to the edge. The wind was stronger up here, and she was having some trouble staying on her heels.

Her stomach knotted, she turned to him. "If you shoot me, your name will come up, you know. You had to swipe your card to get in, so they'll know you were here tonight. You'll be on the list of suspects."

"I wasn't planning on shooting you. Why should I, when you can simply commit suicide?" He glanced over the hip-high parapet. "Poor Agent Fox caved under the pressure. No one would talk to her.

Her director censured her several times. She was about to lose her job, you know. Too bad she took the easy way out."

Renata's mouth went dry as she realized he planned to throw her over the edge to fall to her death on the pavement below. She looked over the low wall and her stomach turned. That was a long, long way down. No one could survive that fall. No convenient awnings or other paraphernalia to break her fall, either, like in the movies.

And he was right. People would think she'd committed suicide…just as her dad had done when his humiliation had been too much for him to bear.

But she wasn't giving up yet, Renata thought, not by a long shot!

"How many people are you going to kill to cover up your…zeal?"

As she spoke, Renata surreptitiously looked around her for a way out.

"The Embry Lake Brigade *had* to be dismantled," he insisted. "Killing Hague's son first was a brilliant stroke. No way would he not order his men to fire on us."

He had her full attention again. "His son? What are you talking about? There wasn't another Hague on the list of dead or wounded. And there wasn't any information on a son in the report."

"Something you missed?" He gave her a mock gasp. "Why, Agent Fox, I'm disappointed. Daniel Griffith wasn't a member of the militia. Of course, given enough reunion time with his old man…"

Renata collapsed back against the low wall. Daniel Griffith…Gabe's brother Danny? It had to be! And if Daniel Griffith had been Joshua Hague's son, that meant the militia leader had been Gabe's father as well. No wonder he hadn't wanted to talk about the man.

And no wonder he hadn't trusted that information to her—a government agent connected with Homeland Security. Even though he'd run from his father and what he stood for, he'd felt tainted by the man. And he'd probably learned to be paranoid early on. He'd probably expected she would arrest him before she would help him. Then when she'd caught on to the fact that he'd been holding out on her, she'd rejected him without knowing all the facts.

And now she was facing death once more…and Gabe didn't even know she loved him.

"So you're responsible for nine people being killed at Embry Lake," Renata choked out, wanting to know everything.

"And not one agent harmed."

She hoped to keep him talking until she could figure out how to get herself free of him. Could she simply run and hide behind one of the air-conditioning units? What then? She had no weapon.

"How many more were there?" she asked. "The five City Sniper deaths—"

"Six, actually. You forgot Muti Hawass. I told you he was on the watch list for association with known terrorists. He hadn't done anything yet that we knew of, but he was ready to act on behalf of his people.

Poor sucker thought he was finally getting an assignment worthy of him when he picked up the rifle and scope."

"So that's how he got it—you left it for him." Renata was amazed at the lengths he'd gone to carry through with his plot. "I don't get it. If you wanted Ackerman dead, then why didn't you simply kill him? Why this elaborate plan?"

"I wanted to shut him up, of course. But he wasn't the only one who needed to be eliminated. There are so many who are a threat to this country."

He was insane. He was playing god with people's lives.

Well, he wasn't going to play god with her life, not if she could help it. She wasn't going to let her death look like a suicide so that the lie could do in her mother and maybe her sister, too, this time. She was going to fight back, and if she went over that wall, she would do everything in her power to take him with her.

"How was Heidi Bourne a threat?" she asked, stalling until she could see an opening. The best she could do was inch away from him and then strike out in hopes of disarming him.

"The Bourne woman made a deal to testify against Congressman Cooper."

"You're working hand-in-hand with him, then."

"Alas, no, I work alone. It's more efficient that way. But Cooper was the head of a committee responsible for creating S.A.F.E. I so admired him for that. I couldn't let such a patriot hang out to dry for a little inappropriate conduct. So I got rid of the Bourne woman and the little prostitute who serviced him on the night in question, instead."

More warped thinking. He didn't see what Cooper had done as a crime.

"What about Maurice Washington and Gary Hudson?" she asked, shifting away from him, subtly putting a narrow margin of space between them. "Why them? Were they connected with Cooper, also?"

"Housecleaning. I figured while I was at it, I ought to remove the personal pariahs in my life. Washington was the source for drugs my kid did. And the reason my wife divorced me. Gary Hudson was her divorce attorney. They both deserved to die."

Renata made her move, but he was ready for her. He blocked her attack and took a step back, then aimed the gun for her head.

"I really would hate to use this and splatter your brains all over the rooftop. If I had wanted to do that, I would have used a rifle with a scope to bring you down long ago. I had so many chances…"

Shaking with fury, Renata thought she must be a fool not to have recognized the clues he'd given her. She'd overlooked them because he'd been the only person who'd given her the benefit of the doubt. But now she knew he'd played buddy-buddy with her to keep tabs on her movements.

How could she not have seen the City Sniper was none other than Agent Paul Broden?

GABE STOOD frozen at the top of the stairs, hoping against hope that he could stop another murder from happening.

Having heard sounds coming from the stairwell as he'd passed it, he'd cracked open the door. Renata's voice had reached him and he'd been hard-pressed to keep his own counsel for the moment. Removing her gun from his pocket, Gabe silently moved upward and then followed them out onto the roof. He kept flat along the building and snaked behind a pipe out of sight.

Renata was saying, "I don't understand why you would have gone after the Embry Lake Brigade in the first place. The tip about the militia working with terrorists came from you, not from some unidentified source."

Broden laughed. "Militiamen…terrorists… what's the difference? We have more than enough of both in this country. Too many for one man alone to clean up. As for the City Sniper victims, they were all undesirables, but it was not nearly as satisfying as simply killing Joshua Hague's son and letting everyone else do the work for me."

Gabe stopped and tried to catch his breath. An admission. The man had admitted to murdering Danny.

Shaking with the need to kill his brother's murderer, Gabe aimed the gun at the bastard's head, saying, "Ackerman wasn't the only one who had it in for you, Broden."

"What the hell—"

"Gabe, get out!"

Broden grabbed Renata and pulled her in front of him as a shield. When she struggled, he merely shoved the gun in her side.

Even so, she yelled, "Gabe, go!"

"I'm not going anywhere, Renata, not without you."

She stopped fighting but Gabe knew she was only waiting for her next opportunity to thwart her captor. Still, knowing Broden would simply shoot them both if he lowered his gun, Gabe refused to do it.

"Ah, such a devoted lover," Broden said.

"You can call me Gabriel Connor. Or Gabriel Griffith. Or Gabriel Hague."

"That's it! I knew I recognized you! You look like your old man."

"I'm nothing like him." Even as Gabe gritted out the words, they rang false to his own ears.

"You have a gun in your hand. I assume you know how to use it."

"I was raised by a Second Amendment fanatic. What do you think?"

Chances were he could shoot Broden between the eyes from where he stood. He would be justified…he would be killing Broden to save Renata's life. But in the end, he couldn't be sure the bastard wouldn't get off a round, as well. Then Renata would die with Broden, and Gabe loved her too much to watch her die.

He had to get Broden's gun away from her and pointed at himself.

That would give her the opening she needed to get free of him.

STILL SHOCKED that Joshua Hague had been Gabe's father and that his brother had been killed so senselessly at Embry Lake, Renata was torn between offering the man she loved comfort and ordering him to get out while he could. The metal muzzle pressed to her side prevented her from doing either, and she feared Gabe would get himself killed trying to be a hero.

What she had to do, then, was find a way to break Broden's hold on her so that she could go for his Glock.

But before she could think of something to distract him, Gabe asked, "So who gives you your orders?"

Broden laughed. "You think I need someone to tell me what to do?"

"Mulvihill does."

"Mulvihill *thinks* he does. He has no clue as to who I really am…or what I've done to safeguard this country. He's a bureaucrat, not a man of action."

"Is that how you think of yourself? As a man of action? A hero, perhaps? That's the way Joshua Hague thought of himself," Gabe said, unable to keep the irony out of his words. "I lived with the man long enough to know that. But you're not half the man he was. I would describe *you* as a lunatic who has gotten sloppy."

The last got to Broden, Renata realized, when he stiffened behind her. She looked at Gabe, but his gaze was focused on his enemy. He didn't spare her a glance, couldn't afford to.

"Sloppy?" Broden yelled. "I got away with ridding the world of more than a dozen undesirables."

"But that's it. You didn't get away with it, now did you?" Gabe taunted. "The greenest new hire at your own agency caught you."

"I'm not the one who's caught."

"You could have fooled me."

"How do you figure?"

"You shoot Renata and I shoot you."

"Then I guess I'll have to start with you!"

Even as he moved the gun away from her side to aim it at Gabe, Renata saw her chance.

She stomped on Broden's instep hard with her high heel, and even as he yelped in pain and loosened his hold on her, she hit the heel of her hand against his gun arm, jerking it to the right. The gun discharged, the bullet going wild.

"Get away from him!" Gabe yelled, and she knew he wanted to take a shot.

"No, don't do it!" she yelled.

Gabe's footsteps slapped against the roofing as he ran toward them.

She struggled against Broden, who still kept a hold on her. He danced away from her feet, so she couldn't get a solid kick in. The best she could manage was to keep his gun hand moving. Then, in desperation and with a great gathering of strength, he threw her off him. Even so, she kicked high and made contact with his arm. The gun went flying and though she tried to duck, Broden caught her in the throat with a glancing blow.

Gasping for air, Renata went down to her knees.

"Renata!"

"Gun…" she rasped out.

Broden dived for the gun, but another blast reverberated through the night and the gun jumped in her direction. Gabe's shot had sent it spinning. Still gasping for air, Renata crawled toward Broden's gun and snatched it.

Broden cursed and ran.

And Gabe was coming for her.

"Broden!" she croaked out, getting to her feet, waving him off.

Without blinking, Gabe switched directions.

Her throat relaxing from the blow, Renata took a careful breath and turned to see Broden clamber onto the wall. What the hell?

"Broden, don't do it!" she yelled.

But her plea went unanswered. Broden jumped. Expecting to hear a scream of agony, Renata only heard a hard thump. And then Gabe was scrambling up on the wall.

"Gabe, no!"

But the words were barely out of her mouth before Gabe went flying, leaving Renata terrified as to his fate.

Chapter Sixteen

Unwilling to let his brother's murderer escape, Gabe had stuck the gun his waistband and had jumped after the bastard. His stomach now did a nosedive as he flew down to the roof of the adjoining building. He landed square on both feet and rolled, then came back up in one fluid motion.

Broden was ready for him with a roundhouse kick. Gabe took a step back and grabbed the other man's foot, but Broden jumped and plowed his free foot into Gabe's thigh hard enough to make him let go. Broden went down, but when Gabe came for him, he kicked out with both feet and caught him in the gut.

Gabe flew back and landed hard. The breath whooshed out of him, reminding him of Renata. He chanced a quick glance back and was relieved to see her looking down from the wall of the S.A.F.E. building.

Then Broden came for him, and Gabe rolled to his feet and straightened, only to meet a fist. His head snapped back and blood spurted from his nose.

Broken…and he didn't feel a thing…must be the

adrenaline. Or the training. Before he'd escaped his father's influence, he'd been taught to take pain. He'd been taught to fight hard and dirty.

He'd been taught to kill…not that he ever had… not yet…

He drove forward, pounded Broden with both fists. The man fought back but Gabe didn't feel these punches either. He had him…the man who had snuffed out his innocent brother's life…and he was too focused to know anything but the burning anger that had simmered in him for months. Without even thinking, he popped Broden's knee as his father had taught him to get the man off balance and turn him just enough to get a blow to his kidney.

"For Danny," he grunted as the man staggered back and hunched over.

Knowing that he would be groggy and helpless— as helpless as Danny had been to stop that bullet— Gabe drew Renata's gun from his waistband and aimed it at the murderer's head. "Danny deserved to live. You don't!"

"Gabe, no!" he heard Renata plead.

He held steady but didn't squeeze the trigger. "Look at me, Broden." He wanted to see the man's face when Broden saw the bullet coming.

"If you shoot him, then you'll be like him," Renata said. "You'll be like your father, justifying any action to get what you want. But I know you're not! You're not like either of them, Gabe! You're nothing like Joshua Hague. Let the justice system take care of Broden."

"I don't believe in the justice system!" he shot

back, trying to hang on to enough anger to do what he had to.

"Then believe in *me*! You told me to believe in myself. I did and we found the killer. Now it's *your* turn. Believe in yourself, Gabe, and in me. I'll make sure Broden pays for everything he did. Just don't shoot!"

Gabe didn't know how long he stood there with his finger on the trigger. He hadn't set out to kill anyone. He'd thought he would help bring down Mulvihill. Nothing had prepared him for facing the man who'd murdered Danny. Nothing had prepared him for this rage.

All his life, the fear that blood would tell had shadowed him. His father had excused the things that he'd done by saying he was protecting them all—his family, the people who followed him, the country, all against the government—when it had simply been an excuse to seize power and put himself above the law.

If he shot Broden—no matter that the man was a criminal of the worse sort—he would be repeating history, the act anathema to the man he had become.

Besides, he did believe in Renata. That woman could do anything she set her mind to.

"Believe in yourself, Gabe!" Renata yelled at him.

Gabe stepped down and felt a horrible dark weight lift from his soul.

WHAT A DIFFERENCE a week can make, Renata thought, as she walked through the S.A.F.E. office to get exuberant greetings from myriad coworkers.

She gave them no more than a polite smile—more than they deserved considering how badly they'd treated her pre-Broden. But here it was, barely a week later. Broden was incarcerated, and the media had acclaimed her and Gabe as the new American heroes.

Gabe…the only cloud on her horizon…they still hadn't settled things between them. They'd been so busy between giving depositions and trying to reassure loved ones that they hadn't found time for each other.

Yet.

She stopped outside Mulvihill's door and took a deep breath. He'd already stopped to see her on his way in, while she'd been typing up what she planned to give him now. In a complete turn-around, he'd not only been ingratiating but had said he'd had faith in her all along.

She'd kept her own counsel and had smiled at him, too.

She knocked and without waiting for a response, walked into the director's office.

"Renata, what can I do for you?"

So it was Renata now rather than Agent Fox.

"It's what I can do for *you*, Elliott."

She'd never called him by his first name before, but he didn't even blink.

"Sit, make yourself comfortable."

He'd never asked her to sit before, either.

"This will only take a minute." She set the folder down on his desk.

"More information about the case?"

"My resignation."

"I don't understand." His expression seemed genuinely confused when he said, "We had some problems, but we're past all that now."

"Yes, we are." She turned to go.

"Wait. Can't we talk about this?"

Renata paused at the door. "The only talking I care to do will be to the prosecutors and the jurors when I testify against Broden. Otherwise, I'm through here."

He was speechless when she left.

As was Gabe when she showed up at Club Undercover that night and told him what she'd done.

"Resigned?" he echoed. "Have you lost your mind?"

"No, I think I found it. I learned so much the last week, Gabe. I hate violence. I really hate guns. And I'm not too fond of the people who turned their backs on me when they were supposed to be watching mine. They should have backed me up, not forced me to bring you into this."

"I see."

They were sitting at the bar. Blade set down a glass of red wine in front of her and winked, then went back to work.

Renata covered Gabe's hand with hers. "No, I don't think you do see," she told him, her nerves tingling at the touch. "It wasn't right involving you, no matter what your background or your reasons. But I don't regret one minute I spent with you." Now her mouth went dry when she said, "As a matter of fact, I would like to spend a lot more time together."

"You would."

She nodded. "*Close* together."

"That can be arranged. How about now?"

Gabe slid off his stool and held out his hand. When Renata gave him hers and stood, he led her to the dance floor and took her in his arms. The deejay was playing a love song. How appropriate. She closed her eyes and thought how good it felt to have those arms around her, how she never wanted Gabe to let go of her.

"Are you sure about leaving S.A.F.E.?" he asked, his mouth close to her ear, his warm breath sending a delicious shiver down her spine.

"Positive. I talked myself into the job because of my dad."

"To follow in his footsteps."

"I thought so at the time. But now I know I had to banish the cloud hanging over our family since Dad died without clearing his name. I wanted Mom and Lucille to be able to make peace with all that."

"You wanted to make peace with it."

"And I finally have. We were in similar situations, Dad and me—disbelieved by our peers, the focus of the media. The responsibility I felt was tremendous, Gabe. I couldn't put a name to it then. I just knew I couldn't fail."

"You didn't."

"Because of you. But now I don't have anything left to prove. I'm free of my ghosts." She looked up into his eyes and felt her knees go weak at what she saw there. "I want to thank you. You made me believe in myself."

"And you returned the favor."

He kissed her softly; her heart swelled and she thought she would be happy doing anything at all as long as it would keep her close to Gabe.

He brushed the hair from her cheek, saying, "And if it wasn't for you, I would have killed Broden. I didn't start out wanting to kill anyone. I only wanted some kind of justice for Danny. I strongly believed Mulvihill needed to be accountable."

"I don't like Mulvihill much and maybe he does need to be accountable for many things," Renata said, "but no one could have second-guessed a Paul Broden, not even him."

"I certainly didn't expect to come face-to-face with the man who killed my brother. I lost it. Danny was eight when we ran, just learning to fight, to use a gun. But he forgot all that. Over the years, he forgot lots of things. The anti-government sentiment and the feeling of separatism we lived with every day. He even forgot how our father used to beat our mother. Not knowing his father ate at Danny, no matter what I told him. He wanted to judge the man for himself. That's why he went to Embry Lake. I couldn't stop him. And I realized that he had to decide for himself what kind of man Joshua Hague was. I didn't think it would get him killed."

"You couldn't have prevented his death."

But Renata knew Gabe felt he should have. She

wrapped her arms around his neck and kissed him, telling him with a brush of lips across lips how much she felt for him.

"So what now?" Gabe asked, sounding a little breathless.

"I don't know. Maybe I could work at the club and become a member of the team."

"I meant about us."

"So did I."

The brilliance of Gabe's smile was reflected in his eyes. "I love you, Renata Fox, and want you to be part of my life."

"Wherever that takes us, I'm ready."

Epilogue

At the bar, Gideon watched Gabe and Renata on the dance floor, while Blade poured glasses of champagne all around—a toast to another job well done.

"Every time we get on one of these cases, someone falls in love," Cass said.

But it sounded more like a complaint than an observation, Gideon thought. "You never know. Next time it might be you."

She answered with a noncommittal "Hmph."

Love, Gideon thought. A fleeting emotion. He'd only loved one woman in his life and didn't expect he would be so foolish again.

The music ended and Gabe swept Renata off the dance floor. Gideon picked up two filled flutes to hand to them, but they kept going, not seeming to see him or Cass or Blade at the bar. They had eyes only for each other as they left the club.

"Well, more for us," Gideon said, handing one of the glasses to Cass and glancing over at Blade. "To another successful case."

Gideon glanced at the exit, but Gabe and Renata had already disappeared, no doubt to spend the night in each other's arms. He and Gabe came from different lives and yet had so much in common that it gave him hope.

If Gabe could find love and happiness in this lifetime, then anything was possible, maybe even for him.

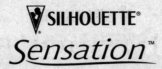

♥ SILHOUETTE®
Sensation™

THE CRADLE WILL FALL
by Maggie Price

Line of Duty

Sergeant Grace McCall still remembered the searing passion she'd once shared with FBI agent Mark Santini. Brought together again on an undercover assignment, the duo had to pretend to be married to catch a killer preying on kids. Would their make-believe partnership turn into a lifetime union…?

'…a spectacular addition to an unforgettable series.'– *Romantic Times*

ALSO AVAILABLE NEXT MONTH

EXPOSED by Katherine Garbera
Bombshell: Athena Force

NOTHING TO LOSE by RaeAnne Thayne
The Searchers

IN HIS SIGHTS by Justine Davis
Redstone, Incorporated

GHOST OF A CHANCE by Nina Bruhns
Shivers

BULLETPROOF HEARTS by Brenda Harlen

Don't miss out! On sale 17th June 2005

Visit our website at www.silhouette.co.uk

Available at most branches of WHSmith, Tesco, ASDA, Martins, Borders, Eason, Sainsbury's and most good paperback bookshops.

Like a phantom in the night comes an
exciting new series from

♦ SILHOUETTE®

INTRIGUE™

ECLIPSE

Beware...there will be a thrilling gothic tale each
month from your favourite Intrigue authors!

Once you surrender to the classic blend of
chilling suspense and electrifying romance,
there'll be no turning back...

MIDNIGHT ISLAND SANCTUARY
by Susan Peterson - *May 2005*

A DANGEROUS INHERITANCE
by Leona Karr - *June 2005*

THE LEGACY OF CROFT CASTLE
by Jean Barrett - *July 2005*

THE MAN FROM FALCON RIDGE
by Rita Herron - *August 2005*

0505/SH/LC112

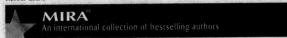

From the *New York Times* bestselling author
TESS GERRITSEN comes a plot that
will make you scream...

ISBN 1-55166-834-3

A ringing phone in the middle of the night shakes
newlywed Sarah Fontaine awake and brings the news that her
husband of two months has died in a hotel fire...in Berlin.
Convinced he is still alive, Sarah becomes embroiled in the clan-
destine world of international espionage, risking everything for
answers that may prove fatal.

'Tess Gerritsen writes some of the smartest, most compelling thrillers around' *–Bookreporter*

On sale 20th May 2005

FREE!

2 Books
and a surprise gift!

We would like to take this opportunity to thank you for reading this Silhouette® book by offering you the chance to take TWO more specially selected titles from the Intrigue™ series absolutely FREE! We're also making this offer to introduce you to the benefits of the Reader Service™—

- ★ FREE home delivery
- ★ FREE gifts and competitions
- ★ FREE monthly Newsletter
- ★ Exclusive Reader Service offers
- ★ Books available before they're in the shops

Accepting these FREE books and gift places you under no obligation to buy. you may cancel at any time. even after receiving your free shipment. Simply complete your details below and return the entire page to the address below. You don't even need a stamp!

YES! Please send me 2 free Intrigue books and a surprise gift. I understand that unless you hear from me. I will receive 4 superb new titles every month for just £3.05 each. postage and packing free. I am under no obligation to purchase any books and may cancel my subscription at any time. The free books and gift will be mine to keep in any case.

15ZEF

Ms/Mrs/Miss/Mr ....Initials..................................
                                                                                    BLOCK CAPITALS PLEASE

Surname ....

Address ....

....Postcode ....

Send this whole page to:
UK: FREEPOST CN81, Croydon, CR9 3WZ